P9-BIX-344

Contact: Spencer Hill Press, PO Box 247, Contoocook, NH 03229, USA
Please visit our website at www.spencerhillpress.com

First Edition: June 2013.

Kimberly Ann Miller
Triangles : a novel / by Kimberly Ann Miller – 1st ed.
p. cm.
Summary:
A teenage girl on a cruise ship to Bermuda wakes each morning in a different reality that may become permanent if she doesn't figure out what is happening.

Cover design by Vic Caswell
Interior layout by Marie Romero

ISBN 978-1-937053-36-9 (paperback)
ISBN 978-1-937053-37-6 (e-book)

Printed in the United States of America

Triangles

Kimberly Ann Miller

Spencer Hill Press

For Jed,
who traveled with me through the Bermuda Triangle many times
and made each trip a great one.

T minus one day to departure for my cruise to Bermuda, I almost died on my way to work.

Should that have been enough to stop me from boarding the ship? Nah.

I just hoped it wasn't some sort of omen.

My best friend and coworker, Nisha, noticed my red face and shaking hands when I punched in. "What's up, Autumn?"

I gulped down a deep breath and sighed. "A giant truck cut me off when I tried to turn into the parking lot, and it almost decapitated me. The only thing that will make me feel better is pizza for lunch. You game?"

She grinned and pulled out her phone. "As long as you're okay, I'll make our reservations right now."

I thought about it for a second. "Yeah, I'll live. Make the call."

At noon, we took our much-needed lunch break at Tony's Pizzeria. I wanted to chat with her one last time, just in case I didn't make it back for some reason—like, I don't know, a sham marriage to some rich dude.

Or death by auto, boat, or serial killer. These days, anything's possible.

"What's your problem, Autumn? You *claim* you almost died today, but you didn't. Why the gloomy expression?" she asked, as my face no doubt sported a scowl.

I looked her up and down and grinned. "Your outfit. Where do you find that stuff?" Even though she was tiny, Nisha stood out like the zit on the tip of her nose. Neon-green spandex tank, watermelon pink miniskirt, and black clunky boots made it look like a garage sale had exploded and she got in the way. Topped off with her long black hair in pigtails, I was almost embarrassed to be seen with her.

Almost, but not quite.

"Hey!" She twirled her pigtails for effect. "I love my style, so lay off. What do you want me to do, be the boring jeans-and-T-shirts kind of girl you are?"

"Touché." I tried to keep a straight face, but a chuckle escaped my lips. "I was just teasing." I glanced out the window smiling, only to frown seconds later. My coworker-slash-shadow had his hands cupped against the glass, his eyes sifting through the lunch crowd inside. "Joey's here." Couldn't I have one damn lunch break without him looking for me? I mean, I knew he had a crush on me, but this was ridiculous.

She rolled her eyes. "What did he leave you this time?"

"A chocolate rose."

"And that rose is—"

"In the trash with the pink rose he left me yesterday." I gulped as I remembered the stench of that flower. It had smelled too much like the ones that had filled the funeral parlor at my dad's service, and our house afterward. The smell of roses always made me think of Dad and my role in his sudden death.

My tears had let Joey know just what I thought of his "gift."

She smirked and leaned toward me. "Was it Godiva? If it was, I am so fishing it out of the trash."

I kicked her under the table. "Can you make me invisible so Joey doesn't see me? I don't want to talk to him now."

She rubbed her shin. "Kick me, then ask for a favor? Kiss off. Here." She handed me a Raspberry Snapple and pulled a Lemon-Lime Gatorade out of her enormous purse.

The pizza guy set our pie down in front of us. Curls of fragrant cheesy steam rose into the air. I took two slices and put them on my plate.

"How do you stay so skinny with all you eat?" Nisha eyed my plate and then my waist.

I rolled my eyes. "The same way you do, Miss Size Two. Good genes."

She chuckled and motioned toward the register. "Did you see that cute guy up there? The short one with the wavy black hair? I've seen him in our store a few times. He's hot!"

I glanced toward the counter. The guy looked over his broad shoulder and caught my eye for a second, smiled, then turned around. He ran long fingers through his hair as he waited for his order to come up. His pressed gray shirt showed off muscular arms. Belted black dress pants accentuated his fit waist and well-built body.

I grinned. "Yeah, he is. I sorta know him. He's the local hottie at the bank on the other end of this strip mall." I sprinkled garlic on my slices.

Nisha's eyes moved from him back to Joey. "I don't bank there. He's a little short, but he's cuter than Joey. From the looks of it, he's richer, too." She waggled her eyebrows. "How do you 'sorta' know him? Something you're not telling me, hmm? Hot banker sex on the cherry wood desk?"

I chuckled and glanced at him before continuing. "His name is Marcus. He asked Jessica out a month ago when she made a deposit at the bank. She said no because she thought he was too young, but he told her he was twenty-one. They went out to dinner, but when he ordered wine they carded him." I bit off a chunk of crust. "Turns out he's only nineteen. Jessica was so mad, she slapped him in front of the waiter! He tried to tell her they'd made a mistake, but she's not stupid. She asked him to take her home, and he actually asked if she was up for some action when he dropped her off."

Nisha gasped. "What a dog! But I bet he's experienced in all things sexual with that face and bod." Her eyes twinkled. "You might benefit from a little of his knowledge. And I don't mean the bank account kind."

I dropped the garlic shaker and waved my hand in the air. Tiny yellow flakes littered the table in front of me. "Take him. I don't need guy troubles."

She drew in a deep breath and sighed. "My mother would kill me if I brought him home. Don't forget, she's happily married to my dad and their marriage was arranged when she was, like, two years old." She shuddered. "If she forces me to marry anyone, I'm getting a sex change operation and calling myself Nick."

I giggled at the mental image of Nisha-as-Nick. So not appealing.

Marcus finally got his order, paid, and walked toward the door with a confident stride.

Marcus arrived at the door just as Joey was holding it for a frazzled-looking lady with three crying kids. I could see the grease on his hands from the oil changes he'd done all morning. When Marcus got to the door, Joey let it go so Marcus had to grab it before it closed on him.

My mouth hung open. "Joey just shut the door in Marcus's face!"

She scoffed. "No way. I've never seen him be mean to anyone." She turned around to see what was going on.

"Agreed. He's not a mean guy. He's actually pretty nice to everyone. But still, he's like that annoying freshman that follows the senior girls around. Even after they tell him to take a hike, he still doesn't get it. And that can cancel out the niceness."

We watched him place his order. At six feet two, Joey towered over the cashier. Everyone could tell he was a mechanic just by looking at his jeans, which were splattered with grease, motor oil, and had torn knees. A red and black bandana drooped out of the back pocket. The S in the Shore Auto on his black logo tee was missing, making the name of the shop look obscene. The always-present pen behind his ear marked a tiny spot of blue ink on his neck.

"Good thing he started going to my sister for haircuts; he looks a lot cuter with his hair a little long and messy like that."

She was right—he did look cute. But his cuteness didn't counteract his annoyingness. "I was thinking about getting a haircut before my trip. What do you think?" I asked as I tugged on my shag, which had been growing out for the past year. "Not that there's much time." I glanced at the pizza-shaped clock on the wall.

Nisha studied my light-brown locks. "I like it at your shoulders like that. Leave it."

I shrugged and chomped down a chunk of cheesy dough. When I looked up, Joey caught my gaze and waved. I pretended I didn't see him. "Doesn't Joey ever take a day off? He isn't the only mechanic we have in this town."

"He won't. Between his deadbeat dad and mom with cancer, I heard he needs the money."

"Yeah, I heard that, too. If I had cancer, I don't think I could deal with all that medicine and losing my hair. I can't imagine being sick all the time, unable to work or hang out with you." And I couldn't imagine anything worse than dying before you really started living.

She gulped down some Gatorade. "Right? Anyway, he's definitely got it bad for you. Remember when he practically followed you into the bathroom at McDonald's?" She giggled. "It's too bad you don't like him.

I bet he'd do anything for you." She tugged her fingers through her hair. "Maybe you could do the 'friends with benefits' thing."

Not this shit again. "Nisha, stop. My life is complicated enough without love or getting knocked up. Besides, I'm getting the hell out of here as soon as I turn eighteen. I don't need a guy holding me back. Even if he's cute or nice or sweet or whatever the hell Joey may be."

She rolled her eyes. "Oh yeah, I forgot. Your plan to 'Get Away from Your Life.' Well, let me clue you in on something, Autumn Rayne Taylor." She took another swig of her yellowish-green drink. "Your problems won't end just because you live somewhere else."

"My Joey problem would. And I could easily just pretend I have no other problems. Lots of people do that." I chugged the rest of my Snapple and set the bottle down on the table. "See? Go away, and the problems stay at home."

"Yeah, you think so? Well, guess what my sister told me?" A wicked gleam in her eyes told me I wouldn't have to guess. "Joey's grandparents are taking him on a cruise." She paused for effect. "YOUR cruise."

My mouth dropped open. "What? Are you sure? Oh my God." I grabbed my ears and put my head down on the cold Formica table. I focused on the crumbs that littered the floor. "This cannot be happening. When did you—"

Joey's booted feet appeared in the center of the crumb collection. "Hi guys. Can I join you?" His usual scent of gasoline and oil did not mix well with my pizza. The smell, along with the news, made me nauseous.

"Uh, I'm leaving. My break is over. You can have my seat." I sat up, rolled the last piece of my slice into the paper plate, and slid out of the booth. "See ya back at work, Nish." I tossed my trash into the can next to our table, dropping my napkin under our booth.

Joey took my place across from Nisha. He pulled the pen from behind his ear and started chewing on the end.

Nisha slapped the pen away from his mouth. It bounced off his teeth with a pop, hit the table, and rolled onto the floor.

"Gross, Joey. Who knows where that pen's been? And I swear, if you pick it up off the floor and shove it back in your mouth, I'm throwing bleach on you."

Joey's cheeks turned pink. He glanced at me and wiped his mouth with the back of his hand. "Sorry, guys. It's just habit. But the pen is clean, I swear. It's mine."

I managed to drag out my napkin with my foot, leaving it at the base of the garbage can, then turned to head out.

Nisha grabbed my wrist before I could walk away. "Tell him, Autumn. Tell him you would never kiss a guy who ate germy pens." She winked at me and giggled.

I knew she was trying to be cute and push Joey on me, but it only increased the distance I wanted between me and him.

My mom chewed on her pens all the time, and my sister Jessica, the perfect nurse, always yelled at her for it. But the germs didn't concern me.

Thinking about my sick mom at the hospital did.

I had to leave before I lost it. I yanked my hand away and rushed out of Tony's. Three doors down, Shore Auto and my crappy job waited for me.

The stink of car parts and gasoline assaulted my nose as I entered the double doors. Despite working there for a few months now, I couldn't get used to that smell, though it wasn't as bad as it used to be. I covered my nose with my hand, then snuck down aisle four, peeled open one of those tree-shaped air fresheners, and hung it on my nametag. Good thing our boss, Colin, was about as observant as a blind mouse. When I slid behind my register and began work, the hours passed in a blur of various customers and car parts. Nisha and I texted between customers, making fun of them to make each other laugh. After one too many teenagers complained about how expensive their bill was, I closed out my drawer in a grumpy mood.

When my shift ended, I put the air freshener back and tiptoed over to the time clock to punch out. When a familiar tall shadow crept up behind me, I cringed. "Joey, I can smell what you did for work today."

He chuckled. "Thank you for pointing that out. A man loves hearing how much he smells like work."

I laughed. "Man? Don't you mean little boy?"

He walked around me and put his arm up on the wall in a pathetic attempt to look sexy. When he leaned, then slipped on a spot of oil, I laughed. He blushed and put his hands in his pockets.

I looked up at him. "You are so not cool." The hopeful look in his chestnut-brown eyes made me sigh. "Joey, what'll it take to get you to stop following me around and leaving me little presents?"

He smiled with white teeth that stood in stark contrast to his olive skin. "Uh, I'm not trying to follow you around, Autumn. Swear." His face reddened. "I was just kind of hoping maybe we could, you know, go out sometime."

Ugh. "Sorry, Joey. I'm leaving Jersey soon and not interested in getting involved with anyone."

He cast a shy glance my way. "That's okay. We can hang out as friends."

"I hear the boss man bellowing for you from the garage." I motioned toward the shop with my chin. "Get back to work. He needs you."

"Joey! This Hummer has to be done in fifteen!" Colin yelled. "Where are you?"

His smile faded and he leaned closer. "Think about it, Autumn. Just say the word, and I'll be ready to hang out with you whenever you want." He sniffed the air. "Do I smell coconuts?"

I grabbed his firm shoulder and pushed him toward the mechanic shop. "Go!"

He stumbled into the garage, and I ran out the front door to hop into my used Ford Escort. On the five-minute ride home, I wondered why Joey was so interested in me.

I wasn't even interested in myself. Must be a character defect on his part.

Two

I parked my car and followed the walkway around into the courtyard. My red-brick apartment building was set up like a square so that all the wooden front doors faced a nice, grassy area, complete with flowering shrubs and trees.

It didn't fool me into thinking I lived in a fancy house.

I'd just gotten my key out of the door when Jessica called out to me.

"Autumn, dinner's ready. And I'd like to talk to you about something."

Wasn't she getting sick of this "I'm your new mom" routine? When we were kids and she helped me tie my shoes or braid my hair or open my Lunchables, I didn't mind her interference so much. Now that she was my official guardian since Mom's accident, it sucked. She asked about my friends, my grades, my "mental status," and even my menstrual cycle. Talk about invasive.

I ignored her and went to my room to change and put my stuff down. I figured I may as well be comfortable when the lecture started.

Sir Sleepsalot napped on my bed. I smoothed my fingers over his silky black and white fur, causing loud purrs to erupt from his fuzzy body. "Love you, little man." I kissed his head and shuffled my now-slippered feet into the tiny kitchen. The smell of hot dogs permeated the apartment. Jessica already sat at the scarred dining room table. Since she was dressed in her Shrek scrubs and had her long blonde hair braided for work, I knew the lecture would be short. Hot dogs and "let's talk" sessions were becoming common in the Taylor household.

I plopped down onto the old vinyl chair next to her, filled my plate with generic potato chips and two hot dogs, and dug in.

"Autumn, we need to talk about school." Jessica poured lemonade into two paper cups. She placed them in front of our plates, then arranged the bag of chips and hot dog buns on the table to neaten the space.

I glanced up at her, then squirted mustard all over my hot dog. The bright yellow color was the exact opposite of my mood. "Save it. I'm not going back."

She sighed, her big green eyes pleading. "You won't get anywhere without a high school diploma. Working at Shore Auto for minimum wage is not going to support you when you're older. Don't you want to go to college, get a good job, be responsible?"

I smirked. "You mean like you? Perfect student, perfect daughter, perfect nurse? Did you ever do anything rebellious or illegal at all?"

She rolled her eyes. "Yeah. I took a pen from work. Anyway, I plan on getting married and having a family one day. You'll want your own life, too, right? And if Mom takes a turn for the worse..." She took a sip of lemonade. "Have you gone to the hospital lately?"

"Yes." What she was asking was if I'd seen Mom lately. The answer to that question was no.

I went to the hospital almost every other day. But I couldn't face Mom. I was the reason she sat in that hospital bed, swollen, pale, full of tubes and wires. I sat in my car, staring up at her hospital room window, until I could no longer see through my tears.

"Good. She'd want you to finish school. So would Dad. You know that."

I forced an exaggerated sigh and slammed down the open mustard bottle. "School just ended last week, Jessica. I really don't want to hear it. And I'll be fine on my own." I swiped a yellow glob off the edge of my plate and licked my finger. "I quit. I'm not going back for senior year and that's that."

"But Autumn—"

I narrowed my eyes. "You're my guardian, Jessica. Not my mother. Leave me alone." I grabbed my plate and cup and pushed my chair back. Lemonade dripped onto my thumb from squeezing my cup too hard. "I'm going to finish eating in my room. See ya." I snatched the bag of chips off the table and stomped down the hall, struggling to hold everything without spilling it all over me.

Footsteps followed me. I slammed the door to my cramped bedroom and locked it. A second later, she banged on it.

"Open up!" She tugged on the doorknob. I watched the knob jiggle from the safety of my messy bed.

"Go away!" I threw a handful of chips at the door, but they gave up halfway there and tumbled to the ground, landing next to the magazine I'd thrown at the door a few days ago. Jessica had a knack of pushing me to throw stuff. "Bye, Jessica. It's time for you to go to work." I quieted down and listened for her retreat.

She smacked the door. "Fine. You'd better pack while I'm gone because we leave tomorrow."

"I'm not going!" I threw another handful of chips. They crunched and scattered as the pile on the floor multiplied. I was close enough to reach down and grab them from the comfort of my single bed, but that would detract from the statement I was trying to make, so I left them.

"Oh, yes you are!" She jiggled the knob a few times. "God, Autumn, why do I bother?"

I heard her footsteps fade as she walked down the short hallway and slammed the front door. The whole apartment shook.

I sighed and focused on a photo of us from when I was five and she was ten. Mom had dressed Jessica as Little Bo Peep for Halloween. I had gotten to be the sheep. Jessica had held my hand all day, had carried my candy, and had proudly told all her friends I was her sister. And when she'd gotten the only bag of Skittles between us, she'd given it to me.

I really missed those days.

Sleepy gobbled down the hot dog pieces I offered. "There's no sense in going back. Sitting in a classroom for eight hours a day isn't going to help me save up enough money to get out of Jersey." October twenty-first could not come soon enough. How many months left till I turned eighteen? Ugh.

I hopped off the bed and checked my bank balance online against the five grand I needed to make my escape.

Three grand short. Great. With the expenses of gas, car insurance, helping Jessica with the groceries, and a little bit of fun, I'd never be able to save enough on my pitiful salary.

I needed a distraction.

I snuck into Jessica's room and grabbed her latest nursing magazine. The images fascinated me, especially pictures of strange rashes. I never told anyone because they would think I was weird. Even Nisha had no idea about my unique hobby. I felt like I was sneaking peeks at porn, but I could already identify a few rashes just by looking at them.

I thought it was kinda cool.

When I finished the mag, I dialed Nisha and asked her to come over and help me pack.

She brought over chai lattes from Starbucks. I had a supply of yellow Gatorade ready in exchange for her assistance. We had the hot and cold covered.

"You gonna hang out with Joey on the ship? He's gonna trip all over himself when he sees your bod in a bikini." She opened one of my drawers and held up a black string bikini I'd gotten last summer.

"No way!" This trip was supposed to be about getting away from it all, not having it all come with me. "And how the hell did he end up booking the exact same cruise as me? It's a little strange, don't you think? I didn't tell him I was going, so he must have been listening to me talk on my phone. My mom planned this, like, two years ago." I opened another drawer and pulled out various pairs of shorts, making two piles on my bed—pack and put away. I pointed to the pile I'd bring with me. "That's what I'm packing."

"Okay. Maybe Joey saw the brochure in your car?" She sipped her chai as she examined a yellow bathing suit I'd gotten the week before. "Jessica could have told him when she had her oil changed, too. Doesn't she chat with him?"

"Yeah, she does. She thinks he's a great future boyfriend for me. She forgets what high school was like with that little puppy dude following you around." With her fantastic looks, Jessica had *every* dude following her around. "But I was careful never to mention the cruise at work."

She laughed, but then looked at the floor and avoided my gaze. My eyes grew wide. "You didn't tell him, did you? I'll *kill* you. No, rephrase that. I'll torture you until you die!"

She shook her head. "No. I swear. But he might have heard me talking at work about wanting to go with you. You never said it was a secret, Raynie."

I threw my hands up in the air. "Great. Now I can have him following me around at work AND on vacation. Lucky me." Maybe I'd jump overboard and disappear. Then Jessica could hang out with him all she wanted and I could be left alone.

Like I wanted.

"Admit it." She poked me playfully. "You think he's cute, even though he annoys you." She held up the swimsuits. "Which one?"

I shrugged. "Yeah, okay, fine. He's cute. So what? I already told you, though. I'm not hooking up with anyone who's going to tie me down. I need to get out of here. And I'll take both suits. Can you grab my cover-up out of that drawer, too?"

She tossed the suits and cover-up in my "to pack" pile. "Ooh la la, Autumn likes Joey! 'Autumn and Joey, sittin' in a tree—'"

I sighed and threw my pillow at her. She ducked just in time to avoid a face shot and laughed.

"Nish, I'd consider going out with him if he wasn't so clingy and needy. I mean, he's the kind of guy who would freak out if I broke up with him. Who needs the drama? Not me."

She shrugged. "What, you don't want to end up on some talk show about your suicidal boyfriend? It's all the rage these days. You guys could chase each other around the stage and watch the bouncer's muscles bulge."

"Ha ha. So not interested, thanks."

"Besides, Joey is the least of your worries. The Bermuda Triangle should top your list of things to worry about on this vacation."

I laughed. "Hardly. I'm not exactly worried about swirling down some massive toilet bowl in the middle of the ocean."

She pulled her fingers through her long black hair. "You joke, but planes and boats go missing, and people think aliens abduct them or they get sucked into a time warp or the military is doing experiments. I've even heard theories about alternate realities, black holes, giant gas bubbles..." She took a deep breath and sighed. "The Bermuda Triangle has been sucking people in for hundreds of years. You might be next."

I laughed. "What a load of crap." A sudden thought lit up my face. "But maybe if I'm lucky, one of those aliens will take Joey. Ya think?"

I shook my head and reached into my closet. When I pulled my sunhat down from the top shelf, a box toppled over and crashed onto my left foot.

"Ow. Shit!" I yelled. I hopped on one foot and glared at the cause of my pain. It was my memory box.

"You okay?"

"Yeah." Not really. I stared at the box, decorated with cat wrapping paper, that held my most secret memories.

"What's that?" Nisha asked.

I turned my back to her so she couldn't see my face turning red and my eyes filling with tears. "My memory box. The one with my Mom and Dad stuff in it. I haven't looked at it in months."

She rubbed my back. "Want a minute?"

I nodded. "Thanks. Can you get out some socks and underwear for me? I'll be right back."

I took the box into the bathroom with me and locked the door. I pulled the lid off and scanned the pile of cards, notes and letters, mostly from my dad. After he'd died when I was little, I'd blamed myself. Like a spoiled child, I'd refused to let anyone sing "Happy Birthday" to me until he arrived. As he sped toward home, he got killed in a terrible car wreck. Since then, I'd collected and squirreled away every single thing I could find that he had written or signed. Old cards, notes left for Mom, anything. Rubbing my fingertip over the indents of his heavy-handed script, I closed my eyes and pictured him standing there with me as he scribbled. I could almost smell his aftershave.

At the bottom of the pile sat the last birthday card Mom had given me. The crease was almost split from being opened and closed so often. "I didn't do it on purpose," I whispered to the cat wearing a birthday hat on the front of the card. "Please snap out of it, so I can tell you that." I was so going to Hell. Killing one parent and almost doing another parent in couldn't possibly look good for me on Judgment Day.

"Raynie, half your socks don't pair up," Nisha yelled from my bedroom.

I replaced everything in the box and went back to my bedroom to pack. I looked for everything on the list Jessica had left for me. "I wish Jessica would stop organizing everything. I can't find the stuff I need!" I dumped out a drawer as I searched for my other bathing suit cover-up. "Get my suitcase out from under the bed, will you?" I asked as my arms got swallowed up in a pile of summer clothes. "I want to get this vacation over with."

"Oh, come on. You could use a little fun. All you do is work and hang out with your stupid cat."

I dumped the pile of clothes on her head. "Sleepy is not stupid! Call him stupid again, and I'll pee in your Gatorade. And you won't know the difference because of that nasty yellow color." I tapped the side of the half-empty Gatorade bottle sitting on my nightstand. "You'd better take great care of him while I'm gone, because if one hair is out of place when I get back I'm coming after you!"

She shook off the clothes and lifted a black lace thong. "Want to take this?" She winked at me. "You never know who you'll meet."

We laughed, but a knock at the front door distracted me. I shot Nisha a glance and ripped the underwear from her hand. She followed behind me as I peeked out the front window.

I sighed. "It's freakin' Joey. I'm not answering it."

He knocked again. "Autumn? I know you're home. Your car's in the parking lot. You forgot your paycheck."

Nisha put her hands on my shoulders and peeked at Joey from behind me. "That was sweet of him," she whispered into my ear. "Open the door."

I pushed her off me and swung the door open. "Hey."

He smiled, but when his eyes diverted to my hand they went wide for a moment. He cleared his throat, then held up the envelope with my check. "Um, you, uh, left this at the garage. I just wanted to make sure you got it in case you needed it, and, uh, I was driving right by."

Oh, goody.

I looked at Nisha. She grinned. I took the check and handed it to Nisha. "Thank you, Joey. But you didn't have to go out of your way just for me."

He shifted his stance and ran a hand through his hair. "It's not a problem. I'm heading over to a buddy's house and you were on the way."

"Well, thanks. I have to go. See you at work." I closed the door.

I spun around to face Nisha. "What was with that stuttering?"

She chuckled, then pointed to the thong I still held in my hand. "I bet he was imagining you in your underwear."

Three

The next day, I dragged that black thong and everything else I'd packed through the port in Bayonne. Jessica led me through the mile-long security line like the travel pro she was.

"This trip had better be worth that inspection." I readjusted my dress after we practically went through cavity searches.

"God, Autumn, can you shut up for one minute and enjoy this? Mom planned this trip almost two years ago. Try to have a little fun. It won't kill you."

After we finished with security and walked toward the monstrous ship, I stopped dead in my tracks. I'd never seen anything like it. The huge white cruise ship resembled a floating city on the dark water. People moved and swayed and hung over sparkling wet railings. A vibe of excitement surrounded the ship, which almost hummed beneath their feet. Balconies with waving families reminded me of the movie *Titanic.* A rock climbing wall jutted up out of the ship and pointed to the clouds above. Seagulls flew overhead, squawking to be noticed and fed. Calypso music, laughter, and the smell of salty ocean water flooded the air.

I closed my eyes and inhaled the humid air, then let the breath out slowly. Maybe I could try to have a little fun. My life had done nothing but suck for a long time now.

"Hey there."

I jumped at the words whispered into my ear and opened my eyes. Standing in front of me was Marcus, the gorgeous guy from the bank. "Going my way?"

Was anyone I knew NOT on this cruise? Weird. I smiled as I drank him in.

Damn, he was hot. He smiled at me with straight teeth surrounded by full lips. Black wavy hair framed his face. Tan Bermuda shorts, a mint-green polo shirt, and flip-flops completed his vacation look. He was about an inch shorter than me, which usually turned me off.

Not today.

"I'm—"

"Marcus," I finished for him. "I know you from the bank. You also went out with my sister, Jessica Taylor, once."

His sexy light-gray eyes betrayed a moment of surprise, but he composed himself and nodded. "Yeah, I remember. That was a while ago."

Really, it was a month. But to a guy like him, that probably *was* a while ago when it came to dating. "She's here with me on the ship. But don't worry, she didn't tell me anything too bad about you." I smirked as I imagined what he was thinking she could have told me.

He ran his hand through his thick hair. "I plead the fifth."

I chuckled and changed the subject. "I've seen you in the pizza place—"

"Yes, you have. And I noticed you, too. You eat there sometimes with your friend and your boyfriend, right?"

I laughed and rolled my eyes. "Uh, no. That would be my friend and my shadow."

His smile widened. He took a step toward me. "Oh! That's cool." He looked at his silver Tommy Hilfiger watch, then glanced around the docks. "Listen, I'm meeting my family shortly. We take this cruise every year for our family reunion. Same week, same ship. A bunch of relatives I don't care about all in one place." He winked at me. "Lucky me."

"Lucky you. I'm Autumn." I extended my right hand out to him. He took it and shook it with a gentle grip.

"Autumn? Cool name. Great to finally meet you." The breeze picked up and carried the scent of Polo from his direction. "Since he isn't your boyfriend, is someone else the lucky guy?"

I raised an eyebrow. "Maybe."

He grinned and pointed at the massive ship that bobbed in the water behind me. "Are you interested in hanging out with me on the ship?"

I smirked. "Probably."

His eyes sparkled at my words. Behind him, Jessica struggled with her carry-on and a handful of brochures. Her digital camera slipped from her wrist and landed on her sneakered foot.

Even though she struggled, she still looked beautiful. Her long, pale yellow hair blew around her face in the breeze, accenting her dark green eyes. Her white cami and barely-there shorts suited her perfect body. People said we looked like twins, but her blonde hair made all the difference. Watching her, I considered dyeing my brown hair to match hers.

"I'd better go help my sister. She's doing a poor job of juggling back there. I'll see you on the ship, then?"

He winked. "Count on it." He waved as he headed toward a group of colorfully dressed people with silver hair. They rushed toward him and hugged him. As I watched, he glanced at me over a tiny gray-haired woman and smiled.

I walked over to Jessica and grabbed some of the papers out of her hand, my eyes still on Marcus. "You know what, Jessica? This might not be so bad after all." When he ran his hand through his hair again, I imagined how it would feel for him to run that hand through my hair and over my body. Goosebumps marched down my arms like a tiny band of ants tickling my skin.

Jessica followed my stare. "Who's that?"

"Marcus, the guy from the bank by Shore Auto. Remember, you went out with him last month?"

She narrowed her eyes in his direction. "Oh, yes, I do remember him. The lying stud."

I laughed. "That'd be him. But he is kinda cute, don't you think?"

She nodded. "Of course. That's why I went out with him, but he's too young for me. If you don't care about the likelihood that he's a player, go have a little fun. But not too much, Autumn. God knows what he's carrying around in those shorts!"

Hmm. I wondered what he had in his shorts, but not the way Jessica was thinking. "Let's get to our cabin and unpack."

"Okay, but Autumn, I want you to lather up with sunscreen. At least SPF 15. And did you bring a hat? I don't want your scalp to burn. Skin cancer's a serious reality—"

I covered her mouth with my palm. "Jessica, be quiet. Breathe. Relax. This is vacation, remember? Can you be my sister instead of my mom for a few days? Please?"

She sighed and grabbed my hand, pulling me into the cavernous main area. I had to hold on tight to keep her close amidst the substantial crowds. Throngs of vacationers, dressed in every bright color imaginable, filled most of the visible space. We snaked our way through to the information center for directions to our room. A gorgeous customer service representative with a plastered-on smile directed us to take an elevator to the ninth floor. When the elevator doors opened, I faced the longest corridor I'd ever seen. Matching cabin doors dotted the length of it. The checkered yellow and green carpet repeated its pattern throughout the hall.

Our room was two doors from the end of the hall. As we walked toward our temporary home, I peeked in some of the rooms as other passengers opened their doors. The rooms were all clones of each other. The only difference was the inhabitants.

"I just dragged my ass a good mile," I said to Jessica as we finally approached Cabin 9666. She sighed and opened the door. Our room was bigger than most of the other rooms we'd passed. I assumed it was because, when Mom had booked it, it was supposed to be the three of us.

I just didn't feel right being here without her. If it weren't for my stupid-ass stunt, she would've been on this ship with us. Storms churned in my stomach as an image of her in the ICU bed spread through my mind like a virus. The mental picture knocked my good mood down a few notches.

I deserved nothing less.

I walked in and dumped my carry-on and purse on the queen bed. The unmistakable scent of coconut made my mouth water. The room resembled a tropical resort with floral bedding, seashell-shaped pillows, beige wicker furniture, and photographs of sea life all over the walls. A television was tuned to a channel that explained what was going on, where things were, and how to get to the ample food and alcohol supply; it blathered on as we scanned our surroundings.

My home for the next five days.

I sat on the bed and pulled out my cell phone. Nisha must have missed me. I already had several messages and texts from her. "I get the bed. You take the pull-out couch."

"How come you get the bed?" Jessica paused in her survey of the room. "I'm the oldest."

I didn't look up from my phone as I answered. "Because I want it. Duh."

She put a hand on her hip. "Well, sorry, Autumn, but that isn't how life works. And stop fooling around with that phone—look at me when I talk to you."

I dropped the phone on the bed and glanced at her. "Okay, fine. I'll give you ten bucks for it."

"Done." She stuck out her hand, palm up, and waited.

Damn, that was easier than I'd expected it to be. I didn't think Jessica could be bought. "Um, can I owe you when I get paid? I don't have much cash on me."

She waved me off. "Forget it. Take the bed. I'm sure the pull-out couch is just as comfortable." She put her purse on the couch and started straightening the pillows. "I'm not arguing with you. Let's have some fun on this trip, okay? I know you're stressed out. I am, too." She sat on the bed and hugged me. "Things will eventually work out. One way or another, they always do. You'll see."

Her hug took me by surprise. We didn't have that kind of relationship. At least, not anymore.

When I was in elementary school, Jessica had insisted that Mom teach her how to braid my hair so she could help get me ready for school. Almost every morning until Dad died, she'd get up early and do my hair, treating me like I was one of her dolls. She even sang to me sometimes. But after Dad died, Mom had a hard time adjusting, and Jessica had to coax her to go to work, cook, and clean.

In helping Mom through her grief, they got closer, and I became just another Barbie doll in Jessica's graveyard of outgrown toys.

The hug brought tears to my eyes. Maybe because I'd been missing Mom. And Dad.

I sniffed the tears back. "Sorry, Jessica. It's just...I don't know. I have so many issues right now I could give one to each person on this humongous ship and still have some left, you know? Sometimes I miss Mom and Dad so much it hurts. Other times, I'm so mad at them for abandoning me, but then I feel guilty for thinking that way."

She rubbed my arm. "I know, Autumn. I know. Me too."

"They were so good together. And the way Mom never dated again after he died, does that kind of love really exist? Because I never see it anymore." If it did exist, I wanted it, but at the same time, having my heart and happiness wrapped up in someone else did not seem like such a great idea. The pain that followed when things didn't work out was just too much to handle.

Jessica gave my shoulders a squeeze. "It's out there. We just have to find it. And we still have each other no matter what, right?"

I laughed and cringed away from her. She wouldn't say that if she knew what I'd done to the car the day before Mom's wreck. Only Nisha and one other girl from school knew.

My boyfriend at the time, Trystan, wanted to see me at the park in the middle of the night. So I snuck out and used Mom's car because I didn't have my own. I also didn't have a license. I picked up Nisha so she could act as my lookout, but on the way to the park, we got stuck in a giant pothole in front of a classmate's house—a girl I couldn't stand named Olivia. After a lot of pushing and rocking the car while Nisha gunned the gas, we freed the car. But it drove like it had square wheels, so we aborted Operation Screw Around and snuck the junker back into its parking space. Since it was driving better by the time I got home, I didn't think the damage was that bad.

But the next day, Mom had the accident that landed her in a coma.

In the car that I'd screwed up.

I tried to disguise my guilt by making a joke of Jessica's comment. "Is that supposed to make me feel better?"

She smacked my arm and got up.

I rubbed my arm and yelped. "Ow! I'm telling Mom!" I spoke the words before I thought to shut up. "Sorry."

Jessica shook her head. "Forget it." She handed me a flyer from the countertop. "This lists the daily activities and times for everything. They have bars—but I had better not catch you in any of them—dance clubs, a spa, a casino, three pools, a skating rink, a rock climbing wall, and all kinds of demonstrations...but hey, don't charge anything to the room without asking me, okay? I have to keep this tight. Our dinner is the late seating, but you can eat at the buffet anytime without dressing up, and you can get room service, too. That's free. Oh, and our room number and dinner table number are printed right on your cabin keycard." She jumped off the bed and walked toward the door.

"Where are you going?" Mild panic touched my voice. After all it took to get to our room, I feared I would be lost forever without her as a guide. I imagined myself wandering down hall after hall for the rest of the trip, knocking on doors and hoping to find Jessica. "I'll never find my way back if you leave me now."

She put her hand on her hip and rolled her eyes. "Relax. I'm going to the bathroom to put on my bathing suit."

She vanished into the microscopic bathroom and shut the door.

My smile faded as I looked at our room number printed on my keycard. 9666. Ugh, I hated those triple sixes. Nisha had once told me that was the number of the Devil.

Why did it have to be my room number?

I glanced out the round window behind my bed. People were all over the dock, smiling, yanking on luggage, and talking on cell phones. No one looked the way I felt. None of their faces betrayed hidden secrets.

I wondered how many of them had almost killed their mothers. Probably none.

I sat there, frowning at the crowd and listening to Jessica sing in the bathroom. Would my life ever get better? Mom had to wake up. I had to talk to her and get over this guilt before it killed me. If she didn't, I'd never get past it. It would burn in me like a candle with an endless wick.

Jessica emerged from the bathroom looking like a fashion model in her floral bikini with dark sunglasses holding back her hair. A towel hung over her arm. "Coming?"

I shrugged. "Will you wait for me? I was going to unpack first, but if you leave and I get lost, what should I do? This ship is huge."

She sighed. "Autumn, we're still in port. Call me on my cell or ask anyone who works here how to get back to our room. Someone will help you. Okay?"

I looked at the floor. "Fine. Go ahead if you're in such a rush. I'll be fine."

"I'll be on the pool deck, checking things out. Just take any elevator to the highest level and you'll see everything. See ya!"

After she left, I unpacked. The ample closet and drawer space in the small cabin held all of my clothes and toiletries with space left for Jessica's stuff. When I was done, I decided to tour the ship, knowing I could reach Jessica if I freaked out for some reason. I considered looking for Marcus to show me around, but I didn't want him hounding me like Joey did if I showed interest. I left the room with my keycard in my pocket and took the elevators to the top level. When the doors opened, I stepped onto a walkway that overlooked the entire ship. I could see the pools and bars below me. "Chaos" was the word that came to mind.

A steel drum band, dressed in Bermuda shorts and colorful Hawaiian shirts, belted out tropical music. Bright sunlight forced me to shield my eyes from the glare off the water. Kids ran around the wave pool, screaming and laughing—noisy reminders to avoid it like the plague. Giant grills cooked up hot dogs and hamburgers. Couples relaxed in a hot tub, resembling lobsters in a boiling pot. A lot of people held books or e-readers in their sweaty hands as they lounged in deck chairs. The lack of sand was the only clue that I wasn't on the beach back home.

I took a deep breath and closed my eyes. The sounds and smells of summer took me back to the time Jessica had to go the emergency room for something in her ear. I was about four, and Dad took me to the shore to walk along the Atlantic Ocean and look for shells while Mom was in the emergency room with her. He sat me on his lap, covered my eyes with salty hands, and laughed in my ear as the cool ocean water washed over our legs. Each retreat of the foamy wave took with it my concern over Jessica. And over getting in trouble. Because no one knew that I was the one who had stuffed the pink Barbie shoe in her ear while she slept. I hadn't planned on hurting her. I just wondered if it would fit.

I smiled at the memory and hoped the Caribbean Sea would do the same thing for my anxiety this time. The only problem was my issues now were much bigger than doll shoes.

My eyes found Jessica, sitting on a lounge chair. She giggled as a guy wearing a navy baseball hat made grand gestures with his hands. The guy stuffed his hands in his pockets and suddenly looked very familiar. In fact, he looked like someone I knew I did not want to see.

Jessica saw me on the walkway and waved. The guy turned, took off his hat, and smiled at me.

All these people on this gigantic ship, and Joey finds Jessica the minute we board? Ugh.

And damn if Joey didn't look great in a pair of jeans shorts and a Yankees jersey. I would have considered hanging out with him, but I knew encouraging him would only make things worse. He would go from hoping to expecting with the first green light I gave.

"I should just plunge myself over the side right now." I marched past countless lounge chairs filled with vacationers. I'd never realized how many different shapes and sizes and colors people came in. Short, fat, tall, thin, black, white, brown, young and old—if the shape existed, it sat in a chair somewhere along my path.

I trudged to the stairs and groaned as I made my way toward Jessica and Joey.

"Hi, Autumn!" Joey practically yelled when I was ten feet away. "Pretty great to know someone on the ship, isn't it? Maybe we can hang out if you aren't busy." His smile carried too much hope with it.

Hope I was about to crush.

"Joey? We just got here. Jessica and I planned on a nice, quiet vacation together. Aren't you here with your family or something?" I crossed my arms. "I mean, I don't want to take you away from your family time or anything." I didn't want to be mean, but I didn't need him hanging all over me from day one.

He played with a loose string on his shirt. "Well, my grandparents on my mom's side surprised me with this trip to give me a break. They set it all up with Colin at work. I—"

"Great. Well, you guys have fun. I'm gonna go check out the spa." I turned to go somewhere, anywhere else.

"Autumn, stay and hang out with us," Jessica said. "We can explore the ship later."

I stopped in my tracks and glared at her. Couldn't she see my need to escape? "I only agreed to come on this trip to get away from it all. It seems that it all followed me here. I need some air." I stalked off the pool deck and ducked inside the first set of doors I could find. Why did he have to be here? I was so being punished for my life choices.

Once I calmed my racing heart, I reviewed a map of the ship. I located the best places to avoid Joey for the duration of the cruise—the library, the art gallery, and the kitchen where they held cooking classes. He didn't read much, didn't care for art, and certainly didn't cook. I made my way to the small library and browsed the young adult titles displayed on the wooden shelves. It was crowded for such a little room and surprisingly well stocked. I wanted to stake a claim on the good ones before we departed. Buying lots of books was a luxury I just couldn't afford, since I needed to save every penny for my escape from Jersey. A few comfy armchairs were arranged in a square around a table full of magazines in the center of the room. I picked up a few books, signed them out, and then headed back to the cabin.

A shrill alarm rang throughout the ship as soon as I got there. I clutched my pillow to my chest and ran to the window. Jessica sauntered in a second later, laughing at my stance.

"Relax, Autumn. I went through this on my graduation cruise a few years back. It's just a life vest drill. Listen to the announcement." She pointed to the speaker in the ceiling.

I strained to hear over the alarm as the friendly woman's words instructed us to grab the ugly orange life vests from our closets and head to the upper decks for the drill. We had to wait till all the passengers were lined up like matches in a matchbox before they inspected us, so the drill took half an hour. Of course, Joey ended up standing behind me. As the line grew, he was squashed into me, but he made sure to keep his hands to himself. I scooted forward to avoid any accidental contact, and ran out of there the minute the drill ended.

I headed to the front of the ship for the departure, avoiding the pool deck and any people who might be hanging out there waiting to annoy me. The sun hung low in the June sky, warming my face with its yellow-orange rays. Seagulls flew overhead, seeking treats dropped by careless passengers. If I hadn't noticed the buildings moving past me, I never would have realized we were in motion. The smoothness of the ship on the choppy water amazed me. How could people get seasick when the ship was so stable?

My hair whipped around my face as we gained speed. I closed my eyes and relished the salty wind on my warm cheeks. A memory of driving with my dad with the windows down flooded my mind. We'd played games in the car for the whole ride that day, looking for license plates from every state and making up silly words out of those plates. When we'd parked, Dad had teased me for the rat's nest my long hair had become. It had been a great day.

I hadn't had a day like that in ages. I missed him so much it physically hurt to think about him. My chest burned and squeezed the breath right out of me, leaving me a breathless pile of misery.

"Are you all right, honey?"

I opened my eyes. An attractive young woman with red hair and brilliant green eyes was looking at me. What I thought was salt water from the ocean must have been tears because my face was the only one nearby that was wet. I glanced at her concerned expression and smiled. "Yes, thank you. I'm fine." I swiped away a tear with my finger. "Just…everything's fine."

She stepped closer and lowered her voice. "This cruise will change your life. Nothing will be the same when it's over, but it will be worth it. You'll see." Her emerald eyes twinkled, and she nodded her head once.

I forced a laugh to be polite. "Thanks. Enjoy your cruise."

What a weirdo. What did that even mean? How could a cruise change my life? I moved from my spot to avoid more weirdness from her and found a less populated area at the back of the ship. New York and New Jersey disappeared behind us as we charged toward Bermuda and away from the mess my life had become.

A cloud covered the retreating sun, sending shivers through me. A white-haired lady dropped her purse and lots of change tumbled out. A penny hit my foot and landed on tails.

My cell phone buzzed. I pulled it from my pocket. I had thirteen messages and thirteen texts. How would Nisha survive the next five days without hearing from me? I took care of the messages and told her I'd call her when we got back to Jersey.

Even though I was not very superstitious, a bad feeling crawled into the pit of my stomach and took up residence.

I knew what I was leaving behind, but what was I floating toward?

Four

I rushed back to my cabin, hoping to leave the bad feeling out on the deck. Maybe the wind would blow it out to sea.

I sat on my bed and opened a novel about a girl caught in the middle of a deadly love triangle that kept recurring life after life. Jessica interrupted me just as the villain was about to kill the main character again. I did a double take at the disaster her hair had become. Jessica never stepped out of the house with a hair out of place.

She smiled at me. I hadn't seen her look that relaxed in months. "Wasn't that departure great? Ah, I love that feeling of wind in my hair as we speed along the ocean." She ran a brush through the tangled mess, perfecting her usual style in minutes. "Dinner is at eight. You coming with me? We have an hour to get ready."

I got off the bed and stretched. "Why not? What should I wear?"

She clapped. "Glad you're coming. A simple dress is fine. I'm going to hop in the shower."

I pulled on a sleeveless navy sundress and flat sandals while Jessica showered. When we were ready, we found the massive three-level dining room at the back of the ship. I felt like I was at a rock concert on the verge of getting trampled as we got close to the restaurant entrance. People pushed their way into the gourmet dinner like this was the first time they'd ever eaten food. I'd never seen so many women with silver hair wearing dresses that sparkled. Was that a required outfit once you hit sixty?

A band of tuxedoed men played jazz music near the entrance. The smell of freshly baked bread and garlic forced a response out of my taste buds, and I had to swallow to prevent myself from drooling. Photographers snapped pictures of the sparkly people like reporters chasing down the breaking news story of the day.

No doubt about it. Cruise ships like to make their passengers feel special.

The maître d' led us through a maze of tables and chairs. I noticed some tables for just two or four people, as well as long and round tables for larger groups. The matching white tablecloths, napkins, and chair covers felt too formal—even in a dress, I didn't feel like I belonged. Crystal wine glasses, real china dishes, and silver utensils sat in perfect arrangements around multicolored floral centerpieces.

"Here we are, ladies. Enjoy your dinner." The maître d' motioned toward a round table with eight chairs. He winked at Jessica, then left.

I turned to Jessica. "Why such a big table?"

She looked away and shifted her weight. "I forgot to tell you. They set a lot of the tables up like the prom or a wedding." She smiled and pointed at the table. "More people means more fun, right?"

I looked at her, then at all the empty seats. Socializing with strangers ranked right up there with going to the dentist as a favorite activity of mine. My gaze moved toward the door. "I'm not hungry." I turned toward the crowded entrance.

Jessica grabbed my arm. "God, Autumn, wait. Please. Just try dinner tonight. If you don't like it, the rest of the trip you can have room service or go to the buffet." She took my hand. "Please? I'll buy you something in Bermuda. I don't want to be here alone the first night."

I let out an exaggerated sigh and pulled my hand away. "Fine, I'll do it just for you. And because I got the bed. But I'm eating and leaving. And I do not plan on talking to anyone, got it?"

She smiled at me and relaxed a bit. "Fine. Just don't be rude, okay? Pick a seat."

I chose a seat leaving my back to the room so I could look out the large windows that surrounded each level of the dining room. I saw nothing but sky and ocean. All of the land had disappeared, and the outside world now consisted of various shades of blues from top to bottom.

I scanned the table. With the number of plates, forks, spoons, and knives I saw in front of me, I wondered how many people were supposed to share the stuff. Then I saw that each person had the same number of utensils. How much did they think we could eat in one sitting?

Jessica sat next to me and put her napkin on her lap. "It's been so long since I've had a vacation. I wish Mom was here. I feel bad leaving her alone at the hospital."

I glared at her. The mention of Mom stirred emotions I didn't want to deal with right now. "Can we not talk about home, please? She's in capable hands, and since she hasn't woken up from her coma in six months, I doubt one week is going to make a difference. Plus, they can contact you if anything happens while we're here."

She glared back. "Autumn, Mom saved up for two years to pay for this trip. You could appreciate what she did for us, you know." She rearranged the glass salt and pepper shakers on the table. I knew her face well enough to see the tears she was fighting to keep hidden.

I slouched in my seat and played with my polished silver fork. "I'm sorry. I do appreciate it. It's just that I feel, I don't know, guilty being here. Maybe this was a bad idea and we should've waited for her to get better." I looked out the window. It may have been my imagination, but every shade of blue I saw before now looked darker. Angrier. More depressed.

The darker colors reflected my bleak mood perfectly.

She opened her mouth again to speak when an old, white-haired couple came to the table. They introduced themselves as John and Mary from Philadelphia. I let Jessica take on the job of playing hostess. I had no plans to remember anyone's names and was sure they didn't care about me. The old lady put a napkin on the seat between her and me, then sat down. Maybe she was afraid to sit next to a cranky teenager. She turned her back to me and busied herself with helping the man put his napkin on his lap.

Next, three round, loud women came and sat across from me. They all seemed to be in their forties, and they all looked alike. They talked way too much. Luckily it was to each other, and not to us.

I rubbed my forehead, trying to silently signal to everyone that I had a headache. I was definitely not returning to the dining room after tonight.

At eight o'clock on the dot, our waiter, Alejandro, came to the table. He handed out leather-bound menus and began explaining the choices in his thick Spanish accent when the old lady next to me stopped him. "Could you wait one minute, honey? My grandson is going to be here any second."

"No problem, Madame." He winked at Jessica before leaving the table. These guys needed a new routine with all the winking going on. Ugh.

I looked at the empty seat with the napkin on it. Great. A little boy sitting next to me for dinner? No way. He would probably do disgusting things like pick his nose and rub it on me or touch my food or insist on talking to me. I shot Jessica a nasty scowl and shoved back my chair to get up. I didn't realize someone was standing behind me until the chair refused to move any further, banging into the person and trapping me.

"Oh, sorry," I started to mumble.

"You're late, honey." The old woman next to me looked over my head at the person I'd just rammed.

"Thank you for pointing that out, Grandma," a horribly familiar voice responded. "Sorry about that. I had a minor problem to take care of."

I froze in place. As soon as I defrosted and pulled my chair back in, Joey pulled out the chair with the napkin on it and sat down. Next to me. His smile was so huge, I thought his face might crack in half.

The only thing preventing me from banging my head on the fancy table was the high chance of stabbing myself in the eye with all that silverware.

Joey leaned over and whispered in my ear. "You didn't have to hit my shin to get my attention. Just being you is enough."

I cringed. What a dork.

He turned and spoke to his grandparents. "I had to dig through the suitcase to find my tie." I stared at him as he fiddled with the ugly red tongue hanging from his neck. He swung his head to face Jessica and me. He couldn't contain that huge smile. "Hi Jessica! How'd I get lucky enough to sit next to you two lovely ladies?"

Um, yeah, and how did I get so *un*lucky? I narrowed my eyes at him. "Did you plan this?" I whispered. "Because I swear—"

He held his hand up to stop me. I noticed the usual grease stains were absent.

"No, Autumn. I told you I had no idea about this. My grandparents set it up." He jerked a thumb over his shoulder. "Blame them." He winked and turned back to the old lady.

I whipped my head around to face Jessica. "Please tell me you did not set this up, because I so do not need this—"

"We didn't even know him when this trip was booked, right? Besides, maybe fate is playing a little game with you. You should listen."

"Hmph." I mumbled under my breath. Fate. Ha. Hadn't fate messed with me enough already? Or maybe this was karma, getting even with me for what I did to Mom. And Dad. And Jessica…

I stole a glance at Joey while he reviewed the menu with his grandparents. In a white dress shirt with the sleeves rolled up and khaki pants that were a tad too long, his hair styled and his cheeks flushed from the heat, he looked pretty good.

A rush of warmth flooded my face and stomach. For the first time ever, I found myself thinking about kissing him, despite his many, many faults. Ugh.

See, just what I thought. This stupid cruise was messing with my mind already. I wondered if it was too late to jump ship. I could swim back to New Jersey and call Nisha to pick me up.

The waiter came back to the table to go over the menu with us and take our orders, but my appetite had plummeted the minute Joey sat down. When the waiter asked for my dinner choice, I stood up.

"I'm sorry. I'm not feeling very well." I put my napkin on my chair and walked out of the dining room without looking back. I could feel Jessica's eyes boring into me, but I didn't care. I knew going on this vacation was a bad idea.

As I rushed to get away from the dining room and its torture, I heard bells and cheers coming from my left. I wandered toward the sound to see what was going on. A distraction would do me good.

I'd never been to a casino before, but there was no mistaking what I saw for anything else. Just like I'd seen in the movies, rows of silver slot machines stood shoulder to shoulder, like soldiers lined up awaiting orders. Card tables, manned by attractive women with big boobs and tiny glittery outfits, held players prisoner to their hopes of winning big. Bells, whistles, electronic voices, and flashing lights lured innocent people into the casino's lair.

"Two grand! I won two grand!" A short man in a green suit screamed a few feet from me. He hugged the slot machine and kicked his feet like a kid getting his first iPhone.

I stood at the entrance, mesmerized by the glitz and the smell of money. A gentle hand landed on my shoulder. "Excuse me, miss. Do you realize you must be at least eighteen to be in here?" a deep male voice asked.

I put my hands on my hips and glared at the security guard. "Of course. I can read. Why do you think I'm standing here watching instead of playing?" I turned with a flip of my hair and walked out.

So much for that get-rich-quick plan.

I wound my way through the ship to the pool deck and up to the stairs leading to the walking track above it. The surrounding darkness prepared to swallow me whole. I walked to the back of the ship and gripped the railing. Stars peppered the moonless sky. The ocean below revealed a smooth surface without traces of life, interrupted only by occasional ripples from the ship. Looking out into the darkness mirrored a look into my soul—dark, empty, lifeless.

The sudden appearance of a family of dolphins caught my eye. Their shiny skin reflected the cruise ship lights like dancing diamonds. I stared with envy as they engaged in a game unknown to me. How I wished my life was like theirs—splashing through the water, basking in the sun during the day, playing with each other. No societal expectations. No familial expectations. No guilt if someone they loved got hurt or died. If I could've jumped in the water and joined them, I would have.

I hung my head over the rail and closed my eyes. The wind rushing through my hair and onto my face blew away my dolphin fantasy. When I heard footsteps behind me, I didn't bother to turn around. I was standing near the walking path, so it was probably some couple out for a starlit stroll.

A low voice whispered in my ear. "Hey there."

I slowly turned to face a gorgeous guy in a suit so black the stars could have gotten lost in it.

Marcus held a hand out to me. "Ready to make your cruise worthwhile?"

Five

I let my gaze drift all over him. "What'd you have in mind?"

Marcus touched my back with a warm hand. "Anything. You game?"

I nodded but didn't speak. He was freakin' hot. He had gelled his dark hair into a purposefully messy style, leaving a small chunk veiling his right eye. The light gray rim surrounding his black pupil resembled a hawk's eye.

Delicious.

He checked me out from head to toe. "Hot tub?"

I'd forgotten I was wearing my dress from dinner until a breeze off the ocean almost lifted it up and exposed my black bikini underwear. I grabbed the hem of the skirt and held it in place.

"By the way, you look fantastic." He spoke in a husky voice.

I wondered just how much that breeze had shown him. "Thanks."

"So, the hot tub? It looks empty." He glanced at the bubbling water one level below.

I grinned, imagining Marcus in a Speedo. "I don't have my bathing suit with me."

He shrugged and gave my body another quick once-over. "Who said we need bathing suits? It's already dark out. No one will—"

"I have to get back to my cabin," I interrupted. I wanted to hang out with him, but with him suggesting skinny-dipping in the hot tub, well, I wasn't quite up for *that*. "I suddenly don't feel that great. I think I ate too much today."

"Okay." He reached out to put a hand on my arm. "I'll walk you to your cabin then. I wouldn't be happy with myself if you never made it there because some other dude decided to make you his."

I smiled. "Sure. It's on the ninth deck."

He stepped next to me and held his arm out like men do in old movies. I hooked my hand in his elbow and started walking. The way he held my hand tight against his muscular chest made my heart flutter. I was grateful I wasn't wearing high heels because, with my flats, we were almost the same height.

"Enjoying the cruise so far?" He pushed the elevator button for the ninth floor.

No. "Yes." I could feel my hand getting damp as it rested in his elbow. "It could be better if…" I trailed off, not wanting to complain about Joey to this guy I'd just met. Listening to people bitch about their exes was such a turnoff. And even though Joey wasn't my ex-anything, it might sound like it to this hottie. I so didn't want him to think that. He'd already mistaken Joey for my boyfriend. Yuck.

The elevator doors opened to reveal an empty car that had mirrored walls. "After you." He released my hand and ushered me inside.

I could feel his stare on my ass as I slipped to the back of the elevator. I turned around in time to catch his eyes wandering back to my face.

He leaned against the rail next to me. In the low light, he looked like a spy with his fancy suit and casual stance. "Tell me, what would make the cruise better?" He tilted his head toward mine so his lips were next to my ear. "I'd love to improve things for you." Warm breath tickled my cheek.

Heat spread through my entire body. Since Trystan had dumped me for not sleeping with him the night I'd taken my mom's car, I hadn't bothered to get involved with anyone else. No one interested me enough to put my heart or sanity on the line again.

But Marcus seemed like the perfect guy to help me back into the wonderful world of dating. Low emotional involvement, high likelihood of fun.

I sighed. "Remember that guy you thought was my boyfriend?"

He straightened and stared at the advancing numbers on the elevator. "He is your boyfriend, isn't he?"

I grabbed his arm. "No! He wants to be, but no. It's not that."

He relaxed his pose and smiled. "What about him, then?"

I put my head in my hands. "He's on this ship with his family. He not only has the same dinner seating as I do, but even the same table." I dropped my hands and looked into his eyes, both now visible in the low light of the elevator. "One of the things I was looking forward to on this cruise was getting away from him, and he followed me. Every freakin' step I take, he's one step behind."

Marcus smirked and ran a finger along my arm. His eyes shone like the glossy silver paint on my boss's Mustang. "I can help you forget your troubles. Just say the word."

I grinned. "I'll keep that in mind." Fantasies of us sneaking into the hot tub together at midnight crept into the back of my thoughts. With bathing suits. At least at first…

He must've been thinking something similar because he grinned and licked his lips. "Okay. Name the time and place. I'll be there."

A fire started deep inside me. This was getting a little too tense. If I didn't step back now, there was no telling what I'd let myself get into.

The elevator doors opened on my floor. I didn't want Marcus to know my room number yet. What if he turned into Joey, the Sequel?

We stepped off the elevator into the nearly deserted hall. I jerked a thumb down the opposite hall from my cabin. "I'm down there. Unfortunately, I'm not really up for anything tonight. Thanks for the company, though. Maybe a rain check?" I turned to walk away and he grabbed my hand. I stopped and looked at him.

He lifted my hand to his smiling lips and planted a long, slow kiss on the back of it. When he looked up at me, that lock of hair had fallen back over one eye. "Goodnight, Autumn. I'll look forward to seeing you when you feel better." He released my hand back to my custody and hopped on the elevator before the doors bumped shut again.

By the time I got to my cabin, I had to jam the keycard into the slot three times before it would work. I flung the door open, threw myself inside, and made sure the lock caught before breathing a sigh of relief.

I stepped out of my dress and tossed it on the floor. The distant hum of the engine filled my ears as I put on an old pair of shorts and a T-shirt. I climbed into bed and pulled the covers up to my chin.

Why was I flirting with Marcus? Why was I attracted to Joey at dinner? What kind of disaster was I setting myself up for?

I was such a loser. If I fell for someone now, I'd never make my escape. My only goal in life would be sabotaged by my stupid, idiotic hormones.

Besides, everyone I loved ended up dead or sick. I didn't want to spread whatever poison ran through my blood to anyone else. Not even Joey.

Luckily, Jessica seemed immune to my toxin with her health, but her life *had* suffered. She was stuck taking care of me when she could be out doing other things like dating, returning to college, or worrying about herself and not me.

Ugh. I was like a disease.

One of Jessica's *People* magazines sat on the dresser next to me. I picked it up and browsed the photos. A picture of a woman looking forlorn made me realize something. Back home, people who knew about my parents always gave me this sad face. It said, "Poor Autumn," and it pissed me off. The whole day on the ship, not one person had given me that face. No one here knew about my dad, my mom, or my life—except for Joey. No one looked at me and felt sorry for poor Autumn and her sister, the girls without parents. They looked at me and just saw a girl.

This was the reason I had to get away from home. I needed a new start. But with this ship crawling with reminders of my past, getting away wasn't going to be easy.

Maybe a fling with Marcus would be a great distraction. Good thing Nisha made me pack that thong.

I checked the time. Already after ten. I put the magazine down and went to sleep.

Blinding sunlight glowed in the window above my bed and woke me. I squinted against the brightness, confused and disoriented. Jessica was sleeping on the couch, her bare legs peeking out from under the floral blanket. Hot pink toenails pointed at me.

Oh, right. The cruise. Marcus. Joey. Images of both guys flooded my disoriented brain.

I stretched and yawned, then glanced out the window. The sun sparkled like crushed diamonds on the deep blue ocean. The sky held no clouds. No other ships shared the vast ocean expanse with us as we steamed toward Bermuda.

I tiptoed around Jessica, threw on some jeans shorts and a pink tank top, and left to explore the ship.

The minute I got to the walking track, I saw Joey and his grandparents. They all had on jogging suits and baseball hats with the ship's logo. How cute. Matching outfits.

Gag.

I was turning to disappear when he called out to me. "Autumn. Hey, Autumn! Great ship, isn't it?" He was breathless from jogging.

I pulled a cat hair off my shirt and watched it float away in the breeze. "I guess. I miss my cat."

He looked down at his feet. "You should try to have some fun. You've been through so much."

I rolled my eyes. Just what I wanted to avoid. Poor Autumn, right in my face, first thing in the morning. I didn't want his pity. I wanted his absence. "Joey, please. I don't want to think about all I've been through, all right? I just want to relax."

He looked at me with compassion in his eyes. "Well, have a nice morning, Autumn. I'm heading to the auditorium. They're having a lecture by the ship's doctor about tropical diseases. It starts in half an hour if you're interested. I could save you a seat."

I put my hands up. "No thanks. I don't want to have to worry about picking up some rash I've never heard of." Though if they had slides, the pictures might be interesting. "Besides, I wanted to spend some time by myself. But, um, thanks anyway for the offer."

He stuffed his hands in his pockets. "No problem. You know, there's no reason to be alone out here on the open ocean. It's supposed to be magical."

"Yeah. Black magic," I mumbled. "Anyway, I have to go meet Jessica. She's waiting for me." I turned and walked away. "Bye, Joey. Have fun."

I continued with my exploration, wandering through each massive deck of the ship from top to bottom. I checked out the pools, the theaters, the restaurants, the photo gallery, the bars, and the library again. On my way back to my room, I passed Marcus on the pool deck. His cheeks already looked sun-kissed.

"Hey there," he said, a bright smile lighting up his handsome face. "Having fun?"

I shook my head. "I already ran into my shadow once this morning, and it's not even ten."

He chuckled. “Can I convince you to join me at the pool in an hour? They’re having a guys-against-girls tug of war in the water. What do you say?”

I turned away with a sultry smile. “I say girls rule. No contest.”

“Want to put your money where your mouth is?” he called as I retreated.

I stopped and turned back to see his dazzling smile beckoning me to play. When he saw me hesitate, he approached. “Change your mind already? Most girls simply can’t resist my charm.” His confident posture told me he wasn’t lying.

I grinned, unsure of what I wanted at this point. “Hmm. Maybe. I’ll be at the pool later. If you aren’t busy with all those other girls, stop by.” I raised an eyebrow and tilted my head just a bit.

I turned and left before he had the chance to respond. When I got back to the room, Jessica was braiding her long hair in front of the large mirror. “Hey Autumn, can you do me a favor and leave me a note or something when you leave the room? I didn’t know where you were.”

I let out an exaggerated sigh. “Really, Jessica, we’re on a ship in the middle of the open ocean. You would have found me sooner or later. Joey has no trouble sniffing me out.”

She finished her braid and started bathing in suntan lotion. “Fine, whatever. I don’t want to argue. Today is our day at sea. I’m going to hang out by the pool all day. If you want, I’ll save a chair for you.” She grabbed a beach bag that overflowed with paperback books. “I’ve got towels, suntan lotion, bottled water, and snacks in here. If you come, bring a book or something to do. See ya.” She shoved her pink toes into flip-flops and slipped out the door.

I pulled on my black bikini, tied the strings nice and tight, and checked myself out in the mirror. Thank God for good genes. I ate what I wanted and still looked good in this little swimsuit.

I hoped Marcus would get to check me out. And Joey wouldn’t.

I threw my clothes back on, grabbed the books and my iPod, and went to the pool deck. Jessica had saved me a chair next to her, so I put my stuff down on the tiny glass table that sat between our chairs and lathered up with sunscreen. She had her head back with her sunglasses and headphones on. Her suntan lotion and magazines sat neatly arranged next to my stuff. I settled into the chair and pulled out a book about serial killers. True crime fascinated me. How any human could do what these people did to other humans boggled my mind. Didn't they ever feel guilt or remorse?

I felt both by the bucketload.

The bright sun on my pages forced my eyes into a squint as I flipped through the black and white crime scene photographs. My sunlight turned to shade as someone stopped at the end of my chair. I snapped my head up to see Joey standing in front of me in cutoff jeans and no shirt. I had never realized how muscular he was, especially in the chest. His hands were already in his pockets.

"Hey, Autumn! Glad to see you out having fun. I saw on the daily report that they're having an ice carving demonstration at noon. Those things can be pretty cool." He sat down at the edge of my chair.

"That sounds like fun." Jessica sat up and started straightening up the books I'd put on the little table. I'd thought she was sleeping next to me with her music on. Guess not.

"Ugh, Jessica, leave the table alone. It's neat enough." She needed medication for her OCD. "Why don't you guys go to the demonstration and I'll watch our stuff? I'm just going to relax today."

And avoid contact with Joey if at all possible.

I could feel Joey's eyes boring into me. "The demonstration is right over there." He motioned toward a covered stage next to the pool. "You can watch it from here if you don't want to get up."

"Well, I'm not interested in that, but I really could use a cold drink right—"

"Say no more." Joey ran toward the bar, tripping over someone's bright green towel and righting himself at the last minute.

"You're so mean, Autumn. How can you take advantage of him like that when you know he worships the ground you walk on? He's got a rough life." Jessica watched him at the bar, sadness etched across her face.

I shrugged. "I figured, as long as he's going to be my shadow, I may as well get something out of it, right?" I scanned the bar and found him leaning against a stool, drumming his fingers on the counter. "Besides, I really just wanted to get rid of him for a little while. He's up my ass like those things you use at work."

She glanced at me. "A suppository?"

I chuckled. "Yup, that's it. That's what Joey reminds me of."

Jessica shook her head and closed her eyes. "That's not nice, Autumn."

I laughed. Maybe it wasn't, but hey, he got under my skin.

"Hey there."

The voice came from behind me. I craned my neck to look back over my seat. Marcus stood over me in a pair of green Bermuda shorts and nothing else.

He walked around to the front of the chair and sat where Joey had been moments earlier. He took a long look at Jessica. Over the years I'd learned that her ability to attract stares exceeded mine. Must be the blonde hair. I rolled my eyes.

When I thought about it, though, I'd never noticed Joey checking her out. Hmm. Maybe something was wrong with him.

What was I saying? There was definitely something wrong with him. I knew that.

"Hey, Marcus. You remember my sister, Jessica?"

"Hi," they said at the same time. Thankfully, neither of them seemed uncomfortable around the other.

He turned back to me and smiled. "Want to go for a swim with me? There's a rule around here that you can't be by the pool without getting wet."

"No there isn't," I said.

He winked. "There should be, don't you think? Come on."

His smile was so inviting, I had to say yes. "Sure, why not?" He reached for my hand.

Joey came back juggling three cups of iced tea as my hand sat in Marcus's. He looked at our hands, then at Marcus. His face visibly darkened. "I was sitting there."

Marcus turned to him. "Not a problem. Autumn and I were just heading to the pool."

I tried to pull my hand from his. "Marcus, this is—" I started to interrupt.

"Come on. The pool is getting crowded." Marcus stood and tugged on my hand. I got up and he released his grip. He slapped Joey on the back as he walked past him toward the pool.

Joey stared at me as I pulled off my tee and shorts. He practically had to wipe the drool off the corner of his mouth. He still held the drinks in his trembling hands, so I reached up to take them. "Give me those before they spill. Thanks for the tea." I set the drinks on the table. Sweat dripped onto my borrowed book. I took a sip and wiped the water off the book.

"Autumn, how can you be interested in him? He's a spoiled jerk." Joey took his drink and shook his head. "He thinks he can buy whatever he wants—including girls. He's going to try to wow you with his money."

"Us Taylor girls don't fall for that, Joey. I've been there," Jessica said.

"How do you know he's a jerk?" I asked, ignoring Jessica. Sure, I'd just met him at the dock. Sure, he'd lied to Jessica. But he seemed decent enough otherwise. And what guy didn't occasionally lie about his age or reputation?

I looked toward the pool. Marcus was standing in the shallow end with his arms spread out on either side of him. His wet hair glittered in the sunlight. With his face turned toward the sun and his eyes closed, he reminded me of an underwear model.

"Because I know him. He treats me like I'm dirt."

Marcus opened his eyes and saw us talking. He waved me over and winked.

"Sorry he's mean to you, Joey. Maybe it's because you slammed the door in his face at Tony's. He's been nothing but nice to me. I'll see you later."

He looked down at my bare midriff. "Um, I, uh, want to taste you." The minute the words came out of his mouth, his face burst into redness. "I mean…." His voice grew with volume and urgency. "I want to race you. In the pool." He continued to stare at my body, now so flustered he was mumbling.

I wrapped my arms around my stomach. "Gross, Joey. I so did not want to hear that. Maybe later. Right now I'm going to hang out with him."

"Thank you for saying maybe. It's way better than no." He glanced at my stomach again, and the redness increased. "Anyway." He changed the subject of my near-naked body and found his voice again. "Marcus is not like us, Autumn. He's a spoiled rich kid. He doesn't know anything about having sick parents like we do or—"

I'd never heard Joey sound so serious before. Maybe he was just jealous that I was giving Marcus more attention than I gave him. "Rephrasing, Joey—you have no claim on me. Butt out."

I left him sitting next to Jessica and walked over to Marcus. I caught him staring at my body as I walked, so I added a little sway to my hips and a little bounce to my boobs, flaunting what I had. He reached up and helped me lower myself into the pool next to him.

"Hey there. Glad you could break away from your boyfriend for a while." He playfully splashed warm water at me.

I chuckled. "He's the shadow I mentioned. I already told you, he isn't my boyfriend."

He scoffed at my comment. "Well he wants to be. It's so obvious. You work with him, right?"

"Yup. We work together at Shore Auto. He's one of the mechanics there, and I work the register."

Joey watched us as we spoke. I felt self-conscious standing next to a hot guy in my bikini while Joey sat nearby. Kind of like I was cheating on him, even though we weren't going out. Every time I caught his gaze, he looked away and blushed.

"He's been after me for a while. I only found out he was coming on this cruise a few days before we left." I laughed. "I almost canceled. He seems to pop up everywhere I go."

Marcus flexed bulky biceps under his tanned skin. "I can take care of that for you. Just say the word."

I shook my head. "No thanks. I can handle myself." Joey's gaze slipped from annoyed to abandoned-cat-in-the-pet-store. I hated the guilt that look brought out in me. I turned in the water so my back was to Joey.

"Tell me about yourself, Autumn. I like your name."

"You can call me Rayne," I said. "It's my middle name, and I prefer it, but no one ever calls me that." I never told people why, but it matched my mood better than Autumn. When I thought of autumn leaves falling, I thought of magic. When I thought of Rayne, I thought of tears.

"How long have you been working at the auto store?"

"Since January. It's okay. My best friend works with me, which makes it a bit more tolerable."

"Is she the girl in the funky clothes? The one you sit with at Tony's?"

"Yeah. She's, um, original, I guess you could say. Personally, I think she just likes to piss her parents off. Her mom's one of those traditional women from India who still believes in arranged marriages." I played with the water in front of me. I had almost forgotten we were in a pool on a cruise ship high above the ocean. "So, you noticed her, huh?"

He grinned and leaned toward me. "I noticed you. A beautiful girl like you is hard to miss, Rayne." He reached for my hand under the water. "I can see why what's-his-name is after you."

"It's Joey, Marcus," Joey said from behind me. "Your brother."

I jumped at Joey's voice. When I turned to face him, my mouth hung open. "Your what?" I glanced at Marcus, then back at Joey crouching next to us on the concrete. They looked nothing alike except for the dark hair. Joey's brown eyes and olive skin didn't match Marcus's gray eyes and light skin at all. And Joey was tall and slender while Marcus was short and built. How could these two opposites be related?

Joey had a wild look in his eyes, but Marcus kept his cool. "Half-brother, Joey. Half. And do you mind? I'm a little busy here with Rayne." Marcus stepped closer to me and put his arm around my waist.

Joey looked at me like he had just found out I was an alien from the planet WTF. "Autumn, what are you—"

I held my hand up to stop him. "You told me to have some fun. I'm doing that. Can I talk to you later? Please? Why don't you go sit with Jessica for a while or something? She looks lonely."

Joey's shoulders slumped. His gaze shifted between Marcus and me. He opened his mouth like he had something to say, then sighed. "Later, Autumn." His eyes shot a death glare at Marcus. He stood and left.

A mischievous gleam entered Marcus's eyes. I unwrapped his hand from my waist and crossed my arms over my chest.

Marcus shrugged. "I didn't bother telling you because we aren't close. We've never even lived together. He's nothing to me, really." He snaked his arm around my waist again. "Don't let him ruin your fun. Doesn't he do that to you enough already?"

Marcus was right. I wasn't going to let Joey ruin my trip or my fun. I figured I would question Joey later, but for now I enjoyed the sinful feeling creeping into my soul. I leaned into his arm. "You realize this changes things?"

"Oh?"

I splashed the refreshing water on my arms and watched the sun glisten on my skin. "Yeah. If you really did notice me, why didn't you ask him about me? If he's your half-brother, you might have asked him to introduce us."

"I told you, we aren't close. At all. I barely know him, in fact. There's no way I could have known he wasn't your boyfriend. And if he ever found out I liked you, he'd try to make my life a living hell for it—like right now." He motioned toward Joey with his chin. Joey sat next to Jessica, arms crossed tight over his chest, glaring at us. "In case you hadn't noticed, he's a little strange."

Yeah, I'd have to agree with that. I cleared the thought and stroked his arm, enjoying the whirls going on in my stomach. "Fair enough. Where were we?" I glanced at Joey again. He was talking to Jessica but still held that guarded pose. "Oh yeah, Tony's. Did you really think he was my boyfriend?" I patted some water on my burning cheeks. "Did I seem like his type?"

Marcus grinned. He looked over at Joey, then back at me. His eyes swept over my body again before he answered. "What do you think? A beautiful girl like you is everyone's type. What concerns me more is, am I your type?"

I didn't really have a type. After Trystan, I pushed all guys from my mind and decided not to get involved with anyone till I moved away. I smiled, refusing to answer. Besides, how could I tell him what I liked in a guy if even I didn't know?

"So, what do you do at the bank?" I asked.

He sprinkled water on my shoulder. "Avoiding my question?"

I shrugged. "Avoiding mine?" Two could play at this game.

"I'm the assistant manager. But I have a secret for ya." He motioned for me to move closer with his finger.

I leaned in till my ear was close to his mouth. His lips brushed my ear as he spoke. "My dad owns the bank."

I moved away and looked at him. "So, are you Daddy's little boy?" I asked, splashing him with warm water. "Rich and spoiled rotten?"

"To the core." He grabbed my hand and held it. His light gray eyes darkened. "Kidding. I do actually work, despite what Joey might tell you about me later. I don't have it as easy as you'd think."

I was acutely aware of the warmth and softness of his hand on mine. I was used to the mechanics and their rough hands whenever they touched my arm or hand at work. Marcus's soft and gentle touch sent butterflies on an expedition through my stomach.

"Hey, Autumn," Joey yelled from across the pool.

The butterflies scattered into the dark corners of my gut. Probably hiding from Joey.

I whipped my head around and shot him a glare. He looked pissed. "What?" I mouthed as I raised my shoulders.

He made it a point to stare at my hand in Marcus's for a second, then he caught my eyes. "Me and Jessica are going to get some burgers for lunch. Want to come?"

Did he not see that I was busy? I shook my head and waved my hand at him like I was swatting a fly away. He looked at our hands again, then walked over to the burger bar without looking back.

Marcus noticed and laughed. "I don't think he's happy you're here with me."

I shrugged. "His problem. He'll get over it." Marcus seemed to like that. He puffed out his chest like he'd just beaten Joey at an arm-wrestling match.

A slim woman walked over to where we stood in the pool. Her slacks and blouse looked like spun silk. The large Kate Spade bag hanging off her shoulder cost more than I made in two weeks. Before taxes. Her face was loaded with makeup. Her hair, perfectly coifed. The smell of money wafted off her through her expensive perfume.

She leaned down next to us and touched Marcus on the cheek. "Marcus, honey, Daddy and I are going to the dining room for lunch. Please join us." She glanced at me like the trash she knew I must be and walked away without waiting for an answer.

Rich bitch. I fought the urge to give her the finger.

"Ha. 'Daddy,'" Marcus said under his breath. He ran his free hand through his hair. "Guess that's my cue to get going. Sabine doesn't wait for anyone."

"You call your mom by her first name?"

He shook his head. "She's my stepmom. She's not that bad, but all she cares about is appearances. Happy family and all that crap."

"Okay." I dropped his hand. "Maybe we can hang out again, Marc."

He leaned toward my face till our wet noses were almost touching. I could feel the heat coming off him. His breath raised goosebumps on my arms. "I like it when you call me Marc. And I'd love to hang out with you again soon. Great to finally spend a little time with you, Rayne." He winked at me with his sexy eyes, lingering close to me for a few seconds. I thought he might kiss me, so I leaned toward him just a little, but he didn't.

I wanted him to. Every nerve in my lips screamed for him to do it. Maybe he was just leaving me wanting more?

It worked.

I watched him glide over to the steps and get out of the pool. Even when he was wading through water, his walk was confident and graceful. I let my legs float up as I relaxed against the pool's edge and let the water carry my weight. The sun settled on my face like my own personal heater.

When I was with Marcus, the things waiting for me back home didn't seem so terrible. Maybe I could have one of those vacation romances everyone always talks about…

Cold water on my arm made me jump. I popped my eyes open and saw Joey holding my sweaty tea glass over my arm. "Joey, what are you doing?"

"I brought your tea to you. Now that your new friend is gone, do you want to have some lunch with us? Jessica already ate her burger, but I didn't. You hungry?"

At his words, my stomach growled. I hated when my body betrayed me. I wrapped my arms around my sides and tried to hide the truth.

"You are hungry. I heard that!" He laughed. "Come on. I'll get you a towel and you can tell me what you want while you dry off."

"Just because Marcus left does not mean I want to hang out with you, Joey." What did I have to do to get him to leave me alone? Get a restraining order?

"But—"

I put my hand over his mouth. "Rephrasing, Joey. I'm not eating right now. Can you please stop following me around? I'll let you know if and when I want to hang out. Okay?"

"I'm sorry, Autumn. I swear I'm not trying to annoy you. I just like being around you." He hung his head, left my tea glass next to me, and walked away.

I got out of the pool and wrapped myself in a large beach towel. I had just sat down next to Jessica when Joey brought over a slice of pizza. "Want a bite? It's good."

I pushed it away. Did I not just say I was not eating lunch with him? I sighed. This guy needed a lesson in taking hints from girls.

"So, what's up with you and Marcus?" He still held the pizza as he waited for my answer.

"What's up with *you* and him?"

He put the slice down on the little table between Jessica and me. His face visibly darkened. "Long, long, very long story." He gestured toward the steaming pizza. "I know you're hungry, whether you want to eat with me or not. Help yourself."

Ugh. He was so hard to discourage. And I was hungry. "Fine, then. Thanks. Can you get me some garlic and salt?"

It worked. He got up and left.

Marcus jogged by ten seconds later. He smirked at me in a way that made me want to leap off the chair and throw him on the ground. In a very inappropriate way. Maybe even eat my pizza cheese off his chest. A grin spread across my lips at the images invading my obviously hormonal mind.

"Have dinner with me tonight?" he asked, a little breathless. He sounded so sexy; I had to clear my throat before I spoke.

I pulled in a breath and smiled. "Look for me after dinner. We can hang out then."

He winked. The look he gave me made me feel like he hadn't eaten in years, and I was the first edible morsel he'd seen. "Sounds great." He pulled his dark shades down over his eyes, hiding his best feature. "I'll hunt you down later." He grinned before walking away.

"Autumn, did I just hear you say you were going to hang out with Marcus after dinner?" Joey asked from behind me as he handed me garlic salt.

"Yeah, so?"

"Please be careful. I don't trust him."

"I'm not worried, Joey. I can handle myself. As you know, I work with a bunch of hormonal guys and hold my own."

He shoved his hands in his pockets. "What's he got that I don't? I just don't understand." He looked at the ground and pouted.

Looks. Muscles. Charm. "Joey, please." He continued staring at his feet. "We already have dinner together. So please stop questioning my plans. I'm going to eat what's left of my pizza and take a nap, okay? I think your grandparents are looking for you." I pointed to two old people dressed in identical white outfits standing on the walkway a level above us. They scanned the crowd and waved to us.

"Guess I'll see you at dinner." He waved back as he headed toward the stairs.

Jessica blinked awake from the tanning stupor she'd been in. "God, you can be so mean, Autumn. Would it kill you to hang out with him for a while?" she asked. "He's obviously got it bad for you."

"Yes, it will kill me. Stay out of it, Jessica. I just hung out with Marcus once, so I don't get why Joey's pestering me about it. I don't want a boyfriend, especially Joey. I just want to get away with Sleepy and forget Jersey and my life. That's not too much to ask." I tossed the garlic shaker onto the table, spilling bits of garlic everywhere.

"PMS, huh?" Jessica laughed and pulled a towel over her head.

Maybe. I brushed the garlic off my book. After I calmed down and finished my pizza, I slept for a few hours in the comforting sun, the breeze and the sound of the waves rushing up to meet the ship lulling me into dreamland.

The dream was sweet. Jessica and me, trick-or-treating as little girls, Mom and Dad smiling at our cute angel and devil costumes. Guess who was the devil?

Thankfully, I'd doused myself in sunscreen before falling asleep or I'd have been red as a giant zit. I woke up sweating with my hair stuck to my cheek. Using my beach towel, I wiped off my face and neck. Jessica's chair sat empty next to me. I scanned the area and found her flirting with one of the hottest guys at the pool. Good for her. She deserved to have some fun.

I unstuck my sweaty legs from the lounge chair and stumbled over to her. The sun shone low in the sky, making everything glow the color of clementines.

I tapped her pink arm. "Jessica, I'm going to get ready for dinner." I glanced at the gorgeous guy and smiled. "Coming?"

She looked at the shirtless stud and giggled. "Go on without me, honey. I'll meet you later. I might be a bit late. Andy and I are going for a dip in the pool."

I turned and scratched my head. Honey? That was weird. Jessica had stopped calling me pet names when I hit puberty a few years back. I had been learning how to use tampons and I'd used up her entire box. She had to run out to buy more and missed a date with her dream guy. I'd apologized, but she didn't talk to me for a week afterward. It was totally my fault, I knew.

But she got me back when she told the guy I liked that I had my period and needed tampon lessons so I couldn't go out with him. "Mortified" cannot begin to describe how I'd felt. Mom had grounded us both for being mean to each other.

Jessica felt bad, but I didn't.

I gathered my junk from the lounge chair, slipped back into my shorts and T-shirt, and went searching for our room. After going down the wrong hall twice, I got lucky and found it. Guess it was true that third time's a charm.

I stood there, checking out my clothes for dinner and wondering if I even wanted to go to the dining room. After all, it meant Joey, lots of people, Joey, being social, and Joey.

Ugh. Jessica had asked me to give it another shot. I didn't think I could handle it.

I followed the crowds to the dining room entrance and waited for Jessica. I didn't want her to worry when my seat remained empty since I didn't plan on staying for dinner. The band was playing on a small stage to the right, so I hung back near them so I wouldn't miss her.

While I waited, I was assaulted by the pungent smell of roses and carnations as a bouquet of flowers appeared in front of me. I grabbed my chest, recalling the smell of the roses Jessica and I had laid on Dad's casket.

I almost ran the other way until I looked up to see Marcus holding the colorful display. "For you."

I forced a smile at him despite my crummy mood. "What for?" I wondered what he was doing here now when he and his family had the earlier dinner seating.

"For hanging out with me. And because they are as pretty as you are." He held his hand over his heart. The expression on his face was adorable. With the romantic music weaving through the air from the band beside me, I got the overwhelming urge to kiss him. Again.

I pursed my lips, wondering why my pulse raced when I looked into his eyes. I leaned a tiny bit toward him, anticipating the feel of his lips on mine…

"Autumn doesn't like flowers," I heard Joey say. He stepped out from the hordes of hungry cruisers. I straightened up and faced him.

"Joey, stay out of my business." I motioned for him to leave with my eyes.

Marcus shot him an incredulous look. "I'm sorry, I don't think you were invited into our conversation."

Joey stepped closer to Marcus. He was almost a foot taller, but Marcus had bigger muscles. I could see Marcus straighten his spine, trying to stand taller himself, as Joey towered over him. Both of their jaws flexed. Both of them were dressed in clean, dark suits.

Things were about to get messy. Because of me. Was I cursed or something?

"Why don't you stop bothering her? She deserves better than you," Joey said.

Marcus took a step closer to Joey. Their chests were almost touching. "Oh really? You mean someone like you?" He looked Joey up and down and chuckled. "A struggling mechanic?" He took a step back from Joey and smirked. "Why don't you leave us alone to discuss this? It's up to her, not you, if she wants my flowers or not. This is between Rayne and me."

I put my hands between them. "Guys, stop!"

A few people in line watched us. The attention made my cheeks burn.

"Leave her alone, or I'll escort you out of here," Joey said. "You don't belong here now. This is our time together." The menacing tone of his voice made my eyes pop out of my head. I didn't know he had it in him.

"Really? I'd love to see you try." Marcus put the flowers down next to him and balled up his hands into fists.

"STOP IT!" I shouted over the music. The band continued to play, but all of their eyes were on us instead of their sheet music. The melody fell off-key, then returned to its classical sound.

"Stop this right now!" I faced Marcus, lowering my voice. "Marc, please. Let me clear this up with him. I'll find you later."

"But I—"

I grabbed the bouquet and handed it to him. He caught the bright flowers against his chest, blinking his eyes as the baby's breath flapped against his face. "Please. I can take care of this. I'll catch you later, okay?"

Marcus looked at Joey, who stood unmoving. He looked back at me. "Fine. I'll find you tonight. I'll be by the hot tub after dinner." He glared at Joey with a sparkle in his eye. "But these flowers are for you. Please, take them." He held them out toward me.

I took them from him and tried not to sniff as the memories threatened to return. "Thank you. They're beautiful," I lied.

He winked at me. "Just like you."

Joey's face was turning darker shades of red with each tick of the clock.

Marcus turned to Joey. "You." He pointed at Joey's chest. "You need to learn to mind your own business. See you soon, Rayne."

He backed away from Joey, but Joey advanced on him. "You're asking for it—"

I grabbed Joey's starched collar, yanking him back toward me. Marcus smirked at him, turned, and walked away from the dining room.

"Hey!" I tried to tighten my grip on his collar. Joey pulled away from my grip and spun toward me. I jabbed a finger at him. "How dare you get involved like that! That had nothing to do with you. Why can't you stay out of my life?" I shoved his shoulder.

The testosterone must have had him pumped up because he didn't back down. He grabbed my arm and dragged me away from the band, pushing me against the wall. He leaned in toward me and lowered his voice. He was so much taller than me that I had to look up to see his face. He was totally invading my personal space.

"You're kidding, right? When he's done with you, when he gets what he's after, he'll toss you aside and move on to the next girl. Can't you see that? I don't want to see you get hurt by a jerk like him."

I poked his chest with my finger. "If I want your help, I'll ask for it. Otherwise, stay the hell out of my life!" I pushed hard and he stumbled back.

I stormed down the hall in the opposite direction from the dining room. A hand shot out of the line and grabbed my arm. I gasped. Jessica stood there, wearing a super-sexy red dress, smirking at me.

We were both silent for a moment. I crossed my arms over my chest and worked hard to calm myself, taking deep breaths and closing my eyes.

She tilted her head toward the site of my drama. "Hey, pretty cool having two guys fight over you, huh?"

"Um, that would be a big fat no." I continued to take calming breaths. "Did you hear that?"

She tossed her head back and laughed. "God, Autumn, who didn't hear it?"

I narrowed my eyes and pursed my lips. These guys were going to be the death of me. If they thought they were going to get into some pissing contest over me, they had another thing coming. I was nobody's property. "I'm not eating dinner. I'm too aggravated. I'll catch you later."

I shook her arm off and continued down the fancy wood-lined hallway. Joey ran up behind me and tugged on my hand.

He put his hands up in surrender as I whipped around and glared at him. "Autumn, I'm really sorry. I didn't mean to start anything. I don't know what got into me." He grabbed his head with both hands. "I don't want to upset you. I just can't stand the thought of him using you. Please, don't be mad at me. When we get a chance to talk, I can explain."

I suppressed a scream. "You're a loser, Joey."

I turned and stalked away.

"Thank you for pointing that out," I heard him say as I retreated.

"Sometimes, the truth hurts," I mumbled.

Seven

With my head on the verge of erupting into flames, I ran to my room and crawled into bed, wrapping my arms around my shaking frame. Sleep hit me like a dive into a hot spring. The rocking motion of the ship offered the best night of sleep I'd had in years. Maybe even since birth.

Around five in the morning, I bolted out of bed. Darkness surrounded me. Jessica lay sleeping on the pull-out couch. Light snores broke free from her rising and falling chest. That was odd. I'd never heard her snore before.

Once my eyes adjusted, I scanned the room using the faint blue light emanating from the alarm clock. Despite my feeling like something was wrong, nothing seemed out of place. I climbed back into bed and looked out the window, but all I saw was dark sea and the hint of morning on the horizon. As I turned away, a flashing light caught my eye. It seemed to be doing that S-O-S thing I'd seen in a movie, but when I rubbed my eyes and looked again, it was gone. It must have been a channel marker or buoy that got lost behind a wave or something. I frowned and crawled under the covers for a little more sleep.

I opened my eyes again when the sun warmed my face around eight. Sleep still pulled at me, but I stretched and yawned it away. My deserted stomach growled. Jessica was on her pull-out couch wrapped up in a pile of blankets, so I tiptoed around her to throw on a pair of jeans shorts and a yellow tank top.

On my way to the bathroom, I tripped and almost broke my neck on the sink. When I looked to see what had caught my foot, I spied Jessica's dress and panties from the evening before in front of the door. Sneakers and sandals littered the floor. The chaotic mess of the cabin shocked me.

She always straightened up before bed. Hell, she straightened up all the time. And now her clothes and shoes were strewn all over and her purse dangled from a doorknob?

Maybe she was drunk for the first time in her life. Maybe she'd decided to take a vacation from her usual Type A personality. At least she was having fun.

I ran a brush through my hair, washed my face, and slipped out the door without waking her.

The extensive buffet served breakfast, lunch, and dinner around the clock. As they finished with one meal, they replaced the food for the next. Any egg, meat, cheese, vegetable, fruit, and dessert I could think of was there. They had a soft-serve ice cream machine, omelet and carving stations, fresh baked bread and rolls, and even sushi. Cruises definitely made sure a girl never went hungry. I didn't even know what time it was when I arrived, but the line for breakfast pushed out the front door. I grabbed a tray and got in line for the omelets.

I filled my plate with fruit, a bagel, and a ham and cheese omelet. A little table in a corner sat near the giant windows that displayed nothing but blue water and sky, so I claimed it as mine. I put my tray down and stared at the waves the ship dragged behind us as my omelet cooled.

"Hey there, sunshine," a voice whispered in my ear as muscular arms wrapped around my waist.

I jumped away and spun around to see Marcus smiling at me. Damn, he was sexy. Wearing a tight black T-shirt and dark jeans, he looked like a short bouncer.

I smiled back. His strong arms around my waist felt good. I was surprised at how he was acting since we'd only known each other a few days.

But I'd been told that the best part of vacation is the fling-with-a-hot-guy, and with Marcus it was looking like I'd soon be able to cross that off my to-do list.

He leaned in to kiss my cheek. Warm lips lingered over my flushed skin.

"Um, want to join me for breakfast?" I asked.

"Of course." He took a bagel off my tray and bit off the end.

My eyebrows pulled down in confusion. "Didn't you get some food for you?"

"Why? You've got enough for both of us. I missed you at dinner last night." He chomped on the bagel, irritating me with the sound his full mouth was making. "Why didn't you come? Everyone asked about you. And you didn't answer your door when I used our secret knock last night. Were you sick?"

My mouth dropped open, and my eyes popped out when he grabbed my banana. I snatched it back before he could unpeel it. "What are you talking about? What secret knock?" And how did he know my room number? I didn't think I'd given it to him yet.

I pulled my tray and the rest of my food out of his reach and scooted away from him. The hurt look on his face confused me. I fixated on his short stature, and I almost swore he'd shrunk an inch in front of my eyes.

He reached across the table to touch my face, but I swatted his hand away. The thought crossed my mind that, at the rate he seemed to want to take things, we'd be engaged by our third date and I'd be knocked up before the wedding. "Marcus, I think you're moving things a little fast, don't you?"

He dropped his hand and sighed. "Come on, baby, you aren't still mad about the other night, are you? Let's just drop it so we can enjoy our vacation, huh?" He grinned and moved around the table toward me.

Oh, shit. It hit me like a migraine. He was another Joey. Did it run in their family? What had I done to myself? I crossed my arms over my chest. I moved again to put the table between us. An old couple at the next table watched as our drama unfolded. "What do you mean, 'our vacation?'"

He reached for an apple on my tray, but I yanked it away from him.

My heart sped up as his antics continued. "Stop touching my food!"

"Come on, Raynie, it's not like they charge you for the apple. If you're still hungry, you can get more."

I regretted telling him to call me Rayne. He stole the apple from my plate anyway, took a bite, then offered it back to me.

I shook my head. "Keep it. You obviously wanted it more than I did."

He dropped his hands and looked at me. His gray eyes clouded over. "Autumn Rayne, we've been through this. I didn't sleep with Olivia. She works at the bank part-time and that's it. I wouldn't ruin what we have for some girl who sleeps with everyone to get promoted. Why can't you believe me?"

I took a step back and scanned the room. Did I miss something? Did I not only wake up on the wrong side of the bed, but in the wrong life, too? "Uh, did I just enter the Twilight Zone or something? What do you mean, 'what we have?' We hung out at the pool yesterday, that's it. I barely know you! You're acting like we're a couple or something."

He came around the table again and grabbed my wrist before I could move. "Don't be like that, baby. I planned this cruise to celebrate our one-year anniversary! Let's enjoy every minute of it. I don't want to fight when we should be enjoying ourselves in paradise." He moved his face toward me like he planned on kissing me, his lips jutting out toward my mouth.

I ripped my wrist from his grip and stepped away from him, shoving on his firm chest at the same time. "You're crazy. I never should've gone to the pool with you," I huffed. "Anniversary. You've got me confused with someone else, Marcus!"

The old people at the next table continued to stare. Marcus whipped his head toward them. "Do you mind?" His voice filled with venom. "Why don't you take a picture? It'll last longer!"

They quickly looked away. I turned to Marcus, my jaw hanging open. How could he be so rude to those people? He was the one acting like a nut, not them.

He advanced on me again, smiling and staring me down. I backed away, cornering myself against the window. "Leave me alone, you freak." I held up two fingers in the shape of a cross.

"Ha, ha. Very funny." He leaned in to whisper in my ear. "You liked this freak last Saturday at the reservoir, if I remember right." He smiled at me and winked. "I still have the blanket in my trunk. Why are you playing hard to get? Or do you just want it to be hard?"

My head started spinning. Maybe I was still dreaming and hadn't woken up yet. That would explain his weird comments and the way he was acting like I was his girlfriend, right? Had I lost my mind overnight?

I pinched my arm. "Ow! Shit!" I was not dreaming.

I glanced toward the exit of the dining room. Marcus had my heart pumping like a caged animal. "Let me rephrase, here, Marcus. We just met! You're nuts. I'm out of here." He started after me, but I slammed on the brakes and held one hand up in his face. "Do not follow me! I mean it!" I left my tray and power-walked to the door. I checked behind me as I made my way through the now-crowded halls to make sure he wasn't following me. I got to the elevators and pushed the buttons for both up and down just to get on as soon as I could. The elevator door opened and I ran in without looking, spun around, and punched the button for the top floor. When the doors squeezed shut, I let out the breath I'd been holding and leaned back against the wall.

Holy shit. What was with Marcus?

Movement out of the corner of my eye startled me. "Gah!"

I snapped my head to the left and found myself face to face with Joey. He had a crossword puzzle in his left hand and a pen in his right, which he had chewed on till it shined with spit.

I held my hand up. "Please spare me whatever comments you're about to make. I can see it on your face. And didn't Nisha already tell you to stop with the pen? Gross."

He blinked a few times, scrunched up his eyebrows, and pulled the pen from his mouth. "I'm sorry, do I know you?"

My jaw fell open. Was this some kind of joke?

"Uh, hello? Joey? We've been working together since January."

Blank stare.

I crossed my arms over my chest. "You've been chasing after me, remember? Hunting me down at lunch? Waiting for me at the time clock? Any of this ring a bell?"

He shoved his hands in his bathing suit pockets and shrugged his shoulders. "Um, I'm sorry, I think you have me confused with someone else. I have a girlfriend." The doors slid open. The elevator was flooded with the sounds of music and laughter coming from the pool.

He pushed past me, a worried expression shrouding his face. "Excuse me, please. Enjoy your cruise."

He scurried out of the elevator and walked right into the arms of the girl I hated most at my high school. Olivia Davis, the only other person who knew I'd stolen and messed up Mom's car.

The bitch had blackmailed me for her silence and forced me to do her Biology homework. She was as dumb as she was mean. How the hell could Joey stand her?

My brain couldn't process what my eyes were seeing. Olivia and Joey? Together on my cruise? Together as a couple? WTF?

When the doors bumped shut, I grabbed my hair with both hands and yanked. I couldn't even push a button to make the elevator move, I was so stunned. I felt my legs lose their strength, so I leaned against the wall of the elevator to support myself.

Sure that I was taking a mental dive, I went back to my room. I opened the door to see Jessica sleeping in the same position I'd left her in. I padded past her and climbed into bed with my clothes and sandals still on. I squeezed my eyes shut and covered my ears with cupped hands and prayed that I would wake up from this nightmare.

Jessica shook my shoulder a half hour later. I cracked open an eye to see what her problem was. "Autumn, come on. We slept in. Time for lunch on the sunny pool deck!" Her voice was chipper as she took her clothes into the bathroom. Through the door I could hear her humming what sounded like a lullaby.

Fear glued my eyelids together. "This morning was just a weird dream," I whispered to myself. "When you open your eyes, it'll all be over." I cracked one eye open and glanced around the room. Nothing looked strange. The out of place clothes and shoes were now gone from the floor.

Thank God. It was just a dream. I stretched and yawned, thanking whoever fixed everything and pulled me back to reality.

"Geez, I had the strangest dream, Jessica." I shook my head to clear it from my mind. I did a few more stretches in bed before pushing myself to a sitting position.

She peeked out from the bathroom with her toothbrush in her mouth. Foam from the toothpaste made her look rabid. "Are you meeting Marcus at the pool?" she asked in a mumble. "He's probably wondering where you are."

I stopped stretching. Why would she ask me that? Maybe because she saw us hanging out and knew I thought he was cute?

I was being paranoid. "I'm sorry, what?"

She rolled her eyes. "Your boyfriend," she said around the foam surrounding her lips. "Are you meeting at the pool or not?"

I stared at her and shook my head, my hands itching to cover my ears once again.

"God, Autumn, what is wrong with you? Marcus? The love of your life? Sound familiar? You missed breakfast, so I assumed you'd be meeting him at the pool. His parents are really nice. I'm glad I got to meet them this trip. And how great is it that they have money! You'll be set with him."

I scrubbed my eyes with the back of my hand before looking at her again. My blood was beginning to boil. "Jessica, is this some kind of joke? Because it isn't funny."

She disappeared into the bathroom again. I still hadn't moved from my spot when she peeked back out. "Really, Autumn, you are so weird. What's wrong with you this morning?"

I sat on the bed, stunned. She couldn't be in on some weird joke with Marcus. She didn't even bother with him after he lied to her about his age. And it was so not like her to care about money like that. She always pushed love back home. Yet here she was, standing in front of me, salivating over a potentially rich husband.

I needed a drink. I was far from an alcoholic, but the few times I drank when my friends had parties, I'd felt so relaxed and calm. So not how I felt now, but definitely how I wanted to feel.

"Um, Jessica, something is in your teeth. Go check it out in the mirror."

While she was busy in the bathroom, I quickly searched the room for her license. She was old enough to drink on the ship. I wasn't yet. But we looked so alike that I could get away with it if I charmed the right bartender into believing I'd dyed my hair brown.

She emerged from the bathroom, catching me opening one of her drawers. "I didn't see anything in my teeth. What are you up to?" She put her hands on her hips. I zeroed in on the space between them. Her abdomen was huge.

Not fat huge. Pregnant huge.

My jaw went slack. Jessica caught me staring. "What?" She rubbed her very pregnant belly with both hands, then smiled. "I know. It looks really big in my summer clothes, doesn't it?"

I shoved off from the bed and got right in her face. "What are you guys doing to me? Is this some sort of plan to make me think I'm crazy?" My heart pounded in my chest. The room no longer felt steady underneath my feet. I crossed my arms over my chest and screamed in her face. "I have enough stress, Jessica! I don't need this right now!"

She pushed her hand against my shoulder and shoved me away. "I don't have time for one of your mood swings. I have enough of my own. Stop acting like a jackass. I'm going to lunch with or without you. I'll see you there if you show up." She grabbed her beach bag and waddled out of the room. I caught the title of one of the books she had in the bag before the door closed. *What to Expect When You're Expecting.* I knew it was a popular pregnancy book because I'd seen it in every bookstore I'd ever been in.

I stood where she left me, fuzziness and fire raging in my brain. It sure didn't sound like she was joking. And that belly did not look fake. Marcus hadn't sounded like he was joking earlier, either. And for Joey to pretend he didn't know me after months of hounding me was just…unheard of. It didn't seem like he was faking it. After staring at him and talking to him, nothing. Not a single spark of recognition.

Did I miss something? Did I forget the past year of my life? Or did I just wake up from a yearlong sleep?

Oh, my God. Maybe I was the one in a coma, not Mom.

I sank to the floor as I considered the possibility. What if my life was not what I thought it was?

Just breathe, I told myself. In, out. In, out.

I closed my eyes and grabbed my head. I rocked back and forth for a few minutes while I tried to figure out what to do.

Feeling like I couldn't deal for a minute longer, I scrambled to the library. Books always provided me with an escape from everyday life. I walked in and calmed my breathing. A young couple giggled in a corner. A man held a little boy on his lap while he flipped through a medical book. A girl who looked to be about ten sat next to him, her eyes trained on the book in front of her. "Dad, what does 'par-a-normal' mean?" She spoke to the man in a thick British accent.

"It means something that can't be explained by science. What are you reading, love?" His accent was as thick as hers.

She didn't look up. "A book about the Bermuda Triangle. I think we're in it now. What are you reading?"

He sighed. Even the sigh sounded British. "I'm trying to figure out what this rash is on William before I take him down to the ship's hospital."

I glanced at the boy and knew instantly. "He has chicken pox."

The father looked at me. "How do you know?"

"My sister is a nurse." And I get a thrill out of looking at pictures of rashes, but I didn't tell him that part.

"My book is seriously cool, Dad," the girl said. "You should see the pictures of the people that disappeared in the Bermuda Triangle."

Could we be in the Bermuda Triangle? Could that explain what was going on?

Ridiculous. I laughed out loud. They both looked at me but I didn't care. The idea was ludicrous, but I had to find out what the heck was happening. Books discussing all things Bermuda lined the wall right behind them, so I pushed past them and read through some titles. A few of them had to do with the Triangle, so I grabbed three and ran back to my cabin. I stuffed the books inside my backpack, along with sunscreen and my room key, and went looking for the information desk.

After getting off on the wrong floor three times, I finally found the busy place. I got in line and felt stupid for what I was about to ask, but what else could I do? I needed answers.

I approached the counter and felt my cheeks get hot. "Hi. I have sort of a dumb question."

The smiling customer service lady stared at me. Her long red hair and green eyes reminded me of someone, but I couldn't place who.

"Are we in the Bermuda Triangle yet?"

She chuckled. "It depends on whether or not you believe it exists, but yes, we did enter the area commonly referred to as the Bermuda Triangle around five in the morning." She pointed to the people rushing every which way. "We didn't disappear or get abducted by aliens, so you should feel free to go on and enjoy your day here on our wonderful ship. Have you reviewed all the great activities we have planned for the day?"

I grimaced at her. "Yeah. Thanks a lot. See ya."

I slunk away feeling like an idiot. I went to the pool deck to look for Jessica and scanned the endless rows of white lounge chairs loaded with bodies. She sat across from where I stood. She was talking to a guy and had her sunglasses in her hair. A book rested on her pregnant belly. He had his back to me, but when he turned his head, I recognized Marcus's handsome face. Oh boy.

I snaked my way through the lounge chairs till I got to Jessica. Marcus was gone by then.

"Hey, what's up?" I asked. Since things were so loopy, I figured I'd take it slow and easy. And if this was just a dream, maybe I'd wake up and it would all be over.

She frowned at me. "You know, Marcus treats you well and you're acting like you don't even know him. What's up with that? You need girlfriend lessons or something."

I looked to either side of her. Both chairs were taken, so I sat down on the edge of hers. She pulled her legs up to give me room. "Jessica, let me ask you something." I smiled a big, fake smile. "What the hell are you talking about?" I blurted. So much for playing along.

"Autumn, look, I'm here to relax. Stop being so difficult. Marcus planned this trip for months. You said yourself he's the most romantic guy you've ever been with. Even Dad likes him."

I shook my head to shake the words around. "Excuse me?"

She waved her hand at me like she was dismissing me. "Oh, come on. You know Dad loves Marcus." Her hands enveloped her stomach. "Zoey's hungry. Would you mind getting me a slice of pizza with everything on it from the pizza bar? No, make that two slices."

I glared at her. Dad was gone. I fought back the urge to throw a frozen drink in her face. Hot tears stung the back of my eyes. "How could you… how could you even bring Dad up? Are you trying to be mean to me on purpose?" I felt my hands shake as the memories flooded my senses.

She sat back in her chair and put her sunglasses on. "You need medication or something. What are you getting all choked up for? If anything, I should be complaining how Dad favors you all the time. God, he makes me promise to tell him where I am at all times, yet he lets you stay out until midnight or later with Marcus. Stop acting so nuts."

I stuttered as I spoke. "But the accident. I…he…" I couldn't finish. I felt the world around me start to tilt to the side. I grabbed the sides of the lounge chair and held them so tight my knuckles turned white. "His car… it's been years since…"

She drew in an exaggerated breath. "What accident are you talking about?"

"The drunk driver," I whispered. "My birthday party…he was hit head on."

She looked into the distance for a second, then recognition lit up her eyes. "You mean that fender bender when his coworker backed into him in the parking lot after lunch? You can be so dramatic sometimes." She waved the waiter over and asked for a virgin piña colada. "You want anything?"

I couldn't respond. Dad had been dead for, like, ten years.

When I didn't answer, she nodded to the waiter to get her order and just shook her head at me.

I tightened my grip on the chair. My knuckles screamed for blood. "How do you know Dad likes Marcus and we've been going out and all that stuff?"

She laughed. "Your little heart to heart chats with Dad are like a reality TV episode. It's not like you try to hide anything." The waiter returned with her frozen, cherry-topped drink. She took a long drag on her straw. Sweat from the glass dripped onto her baby bump. "Are we done? I promised Dad I would finish the books I borrowed from him before I got home."

The tilting world leaned farther to the left. Or maybe it was the right. I didn't know the direction, but I knew my head was on the verge of hitting the ground. "Um, Jessica?"

She huffed and lifted her sunglasses up. "What?" she snapped.

The words pushed through my throat, feeling like gravel. "Dad died in a car accident when we were little," I whispered. It was all I could get out. My head was filled with words that had difficulty reaching my mouth. I felt my lips moving, but no sound came out. Jessica looked at me like I was crazy.

"God, Autumn, did you get too much sun or something? We live with Dad! You're freaking me out. Are you confusing him with Mom? Because Mom died in that truck accident right after you were born, remember?" She must've caught the look on my face, because she added, "Of course you don't remember. I don't remember Mom either, though I wish I did." Her eyes watered as she spoke. "But that's no reason for you to be acting so weird. Are you on drugs? You'd better not be. I'll strangle you. And you'd better not be drinking. You're too young."

I couldn't speak so I just shook my head.

She let out an exaggerated sigh. "If you paid more attention to anyone else at home besides Marcus, you'd remember that Dad paid for this trip out of what he saved from the settlement with the trucking company." She put the sunglasses back on her face and waved me off.

I'd heard enough. I'd seriously gone crazy. I had to go check myself into the cruise ship's hospital.

I tried to get up, but my legs refused to come with me. I slid off the bottom of her chair and smeared my face against the ground. I didn't even have my eyes closed when the darkness pulled me under.

Eight

Coldness on my face bit into the darkness. Jessica's frantic voice snapped me out of my stupor.

"Autumn! What's the matter? Autumn, can you hear me?" She shook my wet shoulder as she yelled, making my teeth bang together.

I felt a finger pressing the inside of my wrist. Coconut and pineapple scented the air around me. My body swayed slightly with the waves. My eyes fluttered open and I found myself sitting on Jessica's chair. Her empty glass explained the smell and the cold. Her piña colada was dripping off my face.

I reached up to wipe my cheeks.

"Here. Let me get that for you, baby," Marcus said. I looked at him and imagined my expression must have looked like Jessica's when I told her I'd quit school. "Jessica, nice job throwing your drink on her face." He laughed. "Good thing it had no alcohol or it would've stung her eyes." He wiped the frost off my face with his finger, sucking the remnants off his skin.

I remained still, closed my eyes, and let Jessica finish checking my pulse. "It's fine. You're fine. What happened? Did the heat get to you?"

It wasn't the heat. It was the things she'd said to me. "Um, I guess so." I kept my eyes focused on the back of my lids. "Can you guys give me a minute?"

"No way," Marcus said, stroking my hair. "We aren't leaving you like this. If you'll stay with her, Jessica, I'll go get her something cold to drink and some food. Maybe it's just low blood sugar."

"Of course. Go ahead. Thanks, Marcus." I heard his wet footsteps slapping toward the bar. "Oh, Marcus, can you bring me a slice of pizza with everything on it? Make that two slices," Jessica yelled after him.

I opened my eyes and found Jessica's rounded face. She looked concerned. Shocked to still see her swollen belly, I reached out and poked it.

She jumped away. "Ow! Why did you do that? Poor little Zoey," Jessica said, rubbing the place I poked. "She didn't mean it, baby girl. Aunt Autumn is just having a bad day."

I shook my head, trying to clear the craziness. Maybe I just woke up from the nightmare of losing my dad and this was my reality. Maybe I was drunk and didn't remember drinking. Maybe someone had slipped me some drug and it was just taking effect.

"You okay?" Jessica asked, wiping the rest of her drink off my neck and right shoulder.

"Um, I think so." At this point, I was afraid to open my mouth and say much of anything. "Thanks."

She looked into the crowd. "Oh, good. Here comes Marcus with a plate for you. It looks like his mother is with him."

Oh, shit. His mother? I didn't even know her and supposedly Marcus and I had been dating for a year? I'd only seen her by the pool the other day and my impression of her was not good. At least I was sort of sick. Playing dumb should be easy.

"Honey, are you okay? You poor thing." The woman I'd seen by the pool yesterday looked at me. Her white tailored shirt and skirt matched the tennis racket she carried.

"Yes, thank you. I'm fine. I have good help."

Marcus sat on the edge of my chair and handed me a plate with garlic pizza on it. "Your favorite."

I took the plate from him and took a bite. It tasted like pizza. And garlic. At least that hadn't changed. Everyone stared at me as I chewed. "I'm fine, you guys. Go have fun. I think it was the heat. Really. Don't waste the day watching me eat."

Marcus's mom checked her watch, glanced over her shoulder, then nodded. "Okay dear. See you at dinner."

I smiled and chomped down another bite of pizza.

His mother left, and Marcus grabbed my hand. "I'm so glad you're okay, baby. We can have some fun now. Just eat and get your strength back. Then it'll be time to play!"

I looked at him, then at Jessica, now rubbing her belly in a circular motion. "Jessica? When is the baby due?"

She exchanged glances with Marcus. "You're kidding, right?"

"Sorry, no. I, uh, forgot." I played with my pizza, pulling the cheese off with my fingers. "Guess this heat is really messing with my mind." I stuffed the cheese in my mouth, getting sauce on the corner of my lip.

"Zoey is due on your birthday, baby. You picked out her name, remember?" Marcus asked. He leaned over and licked the sauce off the edge of my mouth.

Yeah, sure. Remember something that never happened? I didn't even know who Zoey's father was. I swiped the saliva away with Jessica's towel and contemplated what life would be like in one of those mental institutions.

Probably pretty damn good right about now.

Jessica rubbed my shoulder. "I'm going to a cake decorating class, okay? You're in good hands with Marcus." She glared at him and pointed to my slice. "And since he forgot my pizza, I'm stopping for some on the way."

I nodded and took another bite. Marcus stood. "Oh, sorry Jessica. My bad. Can I get it for you now?"

She laughed. "I was just kidding, Marcus. Take care of Autumn. I'll see you guys later."

Jessica struggled against her huge abdomen to get up, grab her bag, and waddle toward the elevators. Marcus sat next to me, leaned back, and closed his eyes.

I finished my slice of pizza. Sudden pressure in my bladder made me squeeze my legs together and get up.

Marcus grabbed my arm. "Where are you going?"

"Relax, Marc, I'm going to the bathroom. I think I can manage it now. I'm okay." As okay as I would admit to.

He relaxed his grip. "Be careful."

"Sorry. I just don't feel that great. I'll be back in a minute."

I went to the bathroom and stopped at the bar on the way back to get a glass of iced tea. Joey walked up next to me and ordered a Coke.

"Joey, have you noticed anything strange going on around here?" I asked.

He glanced at me out of the corner of his eye but didn't answer. He took his Coke and scurried away like a geek being chased by a drunk jock.

Oh, right. I forgot he told me he didn't know me this morning.

Fine, whatever. I looked down to make sure I was still a girl. With the way the day was going, anything seemed possible. All right. Still had boobs. I checked my reflection in the mirror along the back of the bar. I still looked like me.

I watched as Joey walked to a lounge chair on the other side of the wave pool. He handed the Coke to Olivia, then headed toward the diving board.

I approached her and tried my hardest to hold back the urge to toss her over the side of the ship. Her bright-orange bikini top and black bikini bottoms with smiling skulls was as mismatched as her and Joey.

"Olivia?" I said, unsure of what to expect at this point.

She blinked a few times behind her light yellow sunglasses, then glanced around behind herself before focusing on me. She pointed to her chest. "Are you talking to me?"

"Yeah. Do you remember me?"

She squinted her eyes and leaned toward me as if to get a closer look. "No, sorry. Have we met?"

I sighed. "A long time ago, in a galaxy far, far away, I guess. See ya."

I returned to my chair to find Marcus asleep. I sat down, pulled out one of the books on the Bermuda Triangle, and tore through it.

I found lots of information on disappearances but nothing about anyone experiencing hallucinations or mental breakdowns like I was. Maybe other people had gone through it but were afraid to mention it for fear of being ridiculed or put in an institution. Or maybe I was blaming something that wasn't at fault. Thousands of people took cruises through the Bermuda Triangle and had no problems.

I'd finally snapped, just like I'd expected.

I tossed the book onto the table, slammed my head back against the chair and wondered how I was going to survive three more days of this crap if it continued. Who knew what weirdness waited for me on this trip? Hopefully, the next time I woke up, things would be back to normal.

If there was such a thing.

Warm fingers grabbed my wrist. Jessica was checking my pulse again.

"Jessica, I'm fine. Please stop worrying." I shooed her away with my hand. "Is your class over already?"

She dropped my wrist and sat on the edge of my chair. "It was canceled. Not enough people showed up. And Dad said you had to be nice to me on this trip or he was never allowing us to go away again together, remember?"

I jumped up. "No. I don't remember, Jessica. I'm…I…whatever." I plopped back into the chair and hugged my knees to my chest.

I scanned the pool area through teary eyes. A girl who appeared to be about thirteen splashed around with her dad as he held and tickled her wet feet. She laughed and begged him to stop, so he let her go and hugged her.

I hadn't had a good Daddy hug in years.

I would have given anything to have him back. Anything. To undo his death and everything that came after would mean having my parents back. My family intact. My guilt erased. I couldn't even begin to imagine what kind of miracle that would be.

Jessica rubbed my arm. "Sweetie, I have no idea what's going on with you. I wish I could help you somehow. This heat must really be doing a number on you. Should we go see the doctor?" Her hand stopped, forgotten, on my elbow. "I don't do any psychiatric nursing back home, and some of this seems to be, um, in your head. I wish Dad were here. He'd know what to do with you."

Her comment gave me an idea. What if I had the chance to talk to him one more time? I could tell him how much I loved him and missed him and how sorry I was that he died. "Jessica, that sounds great. Can I call Dad?"

She shook her head. "No way. He'll freak out and think we got malaria or something. Why do you want to call him?"

I searched for a normal-sounding answer. "I, uh, forget to send a birthday package out to my, um, Facebook friend." I made this shit up as I spoke, hoping she wouldn't notice the lie.

She sighed. "Okay, fine, but make it quick and make sure to tell him there's no emergency when he picks up. Got it?"

I nodded. "How can I call him?"

"There are phones and computers in the communications lounge on the fifth deck. I mean it, Autumn. Make it very quick. It costs a lot to make a call. And they'll charge it to our room."

"Yeah, fine. I'll be right back. Hold my chair for me."

I got up and she struggled to sink back into the chair. Marcus slept next to us with his mouth hanging open. I checked him out while he slept. He looked great in a deep blue bathing suit and no shirt. His muscles glistened in the sun. Warmth spread through my body and concentrated in the pit of my stomach.

Maybe I should just enjoy whatever was going on and stop fighting it. My whole life was fighting against everyone and everything. I was sick of it.

But the chance to talk to Dad dragged me away from Marcus and his hot bod.

I found the communications lounge and grabbed a phone. I hadn't seen or spoken to my dad in over ten years. I had no idea what to say when he answered. Actually, I had no idea what his number was. Did we even live in that tiny apartment? All I could do was give it a shot.

My heart raced as I dialed the familiar number on the courtesy phone. The white plastic receiver slipped out of my sweaty palm twice before I wiped my hand on my shorts and got a better grip. I took a few deep breaths and waited.

One ring. My heart raced.

Two rings. My legs got weak.

Three rings, then the phone picked up. Tears sprung to my eyes. I dropped into the chair next to me so no one had to scoop me up off the floor if I fainted.

"You have reached the Taylor residence…" Jessica's greeting on our answering machine deflated my anticipation. My heart slowed. I returned the phone to its base and went back to the pool deck, defeated.

Marcus was awake when I got there. He jumped up and gave me a tight hug. The muscles in his arms bulged. Despite my angst over what was quickly becoming my shitty life, I desired his touch.

Any touch, actually. I needed the physical support. "So glad you're okay, baby. Wanna skip dinner with the family and hang out, just us?" he said into my ear.

What the hell. "Sure, why not?"

"Great. It's already near four, so I'm going to tell my parents that we're eating in, okay? I'll catch you in your room later." He kissed me on the cheek, letting his lips linger on my skin. I leaned into him and closed my eyes. He pinched my butt and dashed off.

I couldn't believe it was so late. Jessica had fallen asleep in my chair, so I sat down in Marcus's chair. My life had always been strange, but this was beyond strange. I glanced around the pool area. Kids were laughing and playing in the wave pool. Grown-ups read books and napped in the shade. A belly flop contest was underway in the big pool, sending giant waves over the edge. Everything seemed so normal.

I tapped Jessica's shoulder.

She cracked her eyes open. "Did you talk to him?"

"No, I just got the machine."

She took a deep breath. "Why did you call the house? He's in Paris with his girlfriend, dummy. Try his cell."

I let my head drop to my knees. His girlfriend? Paris?

Three initials ran through my head like a banner on CNN—WTF.

"You know what? I think I will later. I couldn't remember the number. Do you know it offhand?"

She shook her head. "No, it's programmed into my cell. Yours too, I'm sure."

I dug into my bag but didn't feel my phone. Maybe it was in the room. "Thanks. Marcus asked me to skip dinner with him so we can hang out and get room service. Do you care?"

She smiled at me. "Nope. I'm going to dinner in the dining room, then to the show, so have at it. Just be done with whatever you guys are doing by midnight. I won't come back before then to give you some privacy, okay?"

Wow. She sounded kind of cool about the whole thing. Didn't she realize that Marcus could violate me in any number of ways if she left us alone? "Okay, I'm going back to the room to get ready."

She grabbed my hand as I got up. "Just clean up whatever mess you guys make, okay? And stay off my couch! And don't forget about birth control, Autumn. You don't want to have a permanent souvenir from this vacation."

I wrinkled my nose. "Yeah, sure, Jessica. No problem." I gathered my things and headed back to the room. I had enough time for a nap and a shower. The drops of warm water pelting my face felt like bullets trying to pound a message into me.

I must have been on the wrong frequency because I had no idea what that message was.

After my shower, I dug my phone out and scrolled through the contacts. To my surprise, "Dad's cell" was listed.

I stared at the number for what seemed like days. Maybe even years. Then I pulled on my big girl panties, pressed "send," and put the phone to my ear.

My hands shook as I waited for the call to connect, and my stomach quivered as I realized how mad Jessica would be when she got the cell phone bill.

But it went straight to voice mail. And I didn't even get to hear his voice, because he had left the digital, premade message instead of recording one of his own.

I blew out a breath and tossed the phone in my purse. I fell asleep on the couch, thankful for my dreamless nap.

My eyes flew open about fifteen minutes later. Noticing the time, I flipped through my clothes to get ready for Marcus. I pulled on a flirty, knee-length skirt and pink tank top. At a quarter to eight, Marcus knocked on the door.

I opened it to see him standing with an unbuttoned beige cotton shirt, white Bermuda shorts, and flip-flops. "Hey there." He kissed me on the way in, letting his lips linger on mine, then sat down on the bed.

I wasn't so sure about him being on my bed. I hoped he wasn't expecting a sex fest. He was hot, no doubt about it, but I didn't know how far I wanted to take this little fantasy. A vacation fling? Sure. Post-fling consequences and guilt? Sexually transmitted diseases, rashes, babies?

Not so sure.

Pushing things with Trystan had landed my mom in the hospital, not to mention adding to my constant state of suffering. Who knew what would happen if I let things go that far now?

He smiled at me and patted the bed next to him. "Come sit." His sexy smile weakened my resolve. After all, this was all make-believe, so maybe I could screw around just a little without regretting it.

Just a little. What could it hurt at this point?

I walked over and grinned. When I got to the bed, he grabbed the neck of my tank top and pulled me down on top of him.

"Marcus, take it easy." I pushed against his chest and rolled next to him. He moved onto his side and faced me.

His wide, shining gray eyes pulled me into the fantasy. Against my better judgment, I threw my arms around his thick neck and pressed my lips against his.

He didn't need any more incentive than that. He slid his leg between my knees, tangling our bodies together. His hips pushed against my pelvis.

"I'm glad you're in a better mood than you were this morning, babe. You had me worried," he whispered in my ear, then sucked on my earlobe.

I groaned, getting more into it than I'd planned. He rolled me over and slid on top of me, his weight pinning me against the bed.

And I liked it. I ran my fingers through his hair and yanked on a fistful, pulling his mouth closer to mine. His tongue explored my mouth with expert technique. He was the best kisser I'd ever been with.

His warm hand slid up my thigh and edged under my skirt. My hands left his hair and trailed down his back. He rocked his pelvis harder into me and inched his hand higher.

I hadn't been this close to a guy since Trystan. Starved for attention, I grabbed his back with my nails, inviting him to get closer, closer.

His kisses intensified. My breathing increased. All thought ceased to exist as I allowed myself to just feel and not think. I thought too much as it was, letting my brain stop my body from living.

Marcus hooked his finger around my panties and tugged. Releasing my mouth, he nibbled on my earlobe and whispered into my ear. "Do you really need these now?"

I opened my eyes and saw the black lace of my thong peeking out of the drawer I'd put them in, across from the bed.

Damn. Nisha had made me bring them for just this reason, and here I was on the bed with Marcus.

Wearing my ripped Victoria's Secret Pink boy shorts. Why hadn't I thought of them when I'd gotten dressed?

I knew why. Because a sex-fest was not what I wanted. I put my hand on his chest and gave him a shove. This was heading in a direction I didn't want to take.

Yet.

His hand slipped under my shirt, and with one flick of his wrist my boobs escaped from my unclasped bra.

I rolled away from him. "Marcus, please, take it easy." I struggled to get up and hook my bra. I knew he got around, but his expert technique at getting to my goodies with the twist of his wrist only served as a reminder that being with him could equal a trip to the gynecologist.

And a few swabs and antibiotics.

He laughed at me and clutched my waist. "Come on, baby! You told me Jessica said she was leaving us alone for the night. We have until midnight to do all the crazy things we want!"

"Please stop. I'm not in the mood for this right now. I'm…really hungry. And still woozy from fainting earlier. Maybe we can get back to this later?"

He released me and lay back on the bed. I stood and straightened out my shirt. He folded his arms under his head and grinned at me. "Only if you promise me a rain check."

God, he was so damn sexy. I needed to get my act together before I did something I regretted. I guess I missed having a guy around more than I thought I did.

"I thought we were getting together for dinner," I stammered, trying to douse the flames. His and mine. "Let's order something."

He sat up. "Sure, we can order if you want. Go ahead and pick something and I'll keep you busy while we wait." He got up and started nibbling on my neck.

I ducked out from under him and rubbed my neck. "You know what? How about the buffet?"

He wrapped his arm around my waist and sighed. "Whatever you want, baby. Let's go."

I breathed a sigh of relief and grabbed my little leather purse. I didn't want to stay in my room alone with him when he obviously had sex on his mind. And it wasn't far from mine, either. But I wasn't about to sleep with him now, not while everything was so crazy and I had no idea what was real. My body wanted to, but thankfully my brain was still intact and told my body to get a grip.

On second thought, thinking was a good idea.

We went to the buffet and filled our plates with turkey, mashed potatoes, bread, and cranberry sauce. Marcus found a quiet table in the corner of the room, hidden from view and dimly lit.

I took a bite of turkey. "Marc, I can't remember who the father of Jessica's baby is." I circled my finger around my ear. "Too much sun."

Marcus looked at me like I'd grown a third boob. His face clouded over. "Are you okay? I think you might need to see the doctor or something." He reached across the table and put his hand on my forehead.

I picked up a dinner roll and pulled it apart. "Hmm. Maybe." I knew I needed the doctor. But the doctor wouldn't be able to answer my question now. "Just humor me, hon. Who's Zoey's father?"

His face contorted in confusion. "Andy died, remember?"

I continued to stare at him like his words didn't translate into the English I had been taught. "Andy?" I never knew her to date a guy named Andy. "Andy died?" I banged on the side of my head a few times to indicate I needed to shake the memory loose.

Marcus scooted his chair closer to mine. "Jessica and Andy worked together at the hospital. They got married, and soon after, she got pregnant." Marcus took my hand in his, lightly rubbing his thumb over my knuckles. "Andy had skin cancer and died three months after he found out. Melanoma or something like that. It was hiding under his hair, on his scalp. Remember, we all got checked after that?" He squeezed my hand. "You sure you're okay?"

Wow. Dead of cancer in his twenties. He would miss out on so much—his baby growing up, traveling, growing old with Jessica. How sad. I fought back the moisture pooling in my eyes.

The iced tea I sipped slid down my chin. I grabbed a napkin. "How has Jessica been handling it?"

He shook his head and resumed eating. "You did have too much sun. Anyway, new subject. I hate this serious stuff. What do you want to do in Bermuda?"

I slopped a chunk of butter onto my roll. "I don't know. Maybe jump off a cliff?"

He chuckled. I picked at my food and tried to figure out ways to get out of this Twilight Zone. I had no idea how it had started, so how could I end it? What if it lasted the whole trip? Or longer?

I glanced up at Marcus while I ate. Though he had a great body and obviously enjoyed making out, which he was great at, he didn't have much of anything interesting to say. Football, soccer, baseball, and wrestling. Who cares? Not me. I'd had better conversations with Joey at the time clock.

That was saying a lot.

When Marcus finished his third plate of food, he sat back and sighed. "That was great." He rubbed his swollen stomach.

"Yeah. The food on this ship is fantastic."

He moved closer to me and ran his hand up my thigh. "You know what else is fantastic? Your body."

I pulled away and glared at him. "Don't say things like that, Marcus. We're in the dining room."

"So what? You love it, and you know it. And when we get back to the room, I'm going to do that thing with my tongue that drives you wild. How about that?" He waggled his eyebrows at me and reached his hand dangerously close to my panties. Again.

I pushed his hand away, stood up, and dumped my plate on him.

How about that?

Though the image of Marcus dripping with slick turkey gravy and cranberry sauce was funny on some level, I was pissed and confused. I must be in Hell. It was the only explanation. Maybe I could talk to the Bermuda Triangle people or organization or whatever and tell them that I figured the mystery out.

The Triangle led you to your own personal Hell.

It was time to see the doctor. I left the dining hall and ran to the information desk that I'd visited earlier.

"Can I help you?" a pretty, fair-skinned woman asked.

"Yes, please. Can you tell me how to get to the ship's doctor? I need to be seen."

She looked at her thin silver watch. "Is this an emergency? The doctor's office is usually closed at this time."

"Yes. It's an emergency."

She looked at her watch again, then dialed the phone. After a ten-second conversation with the mouthpiece, she hung up and nodded. "Okay, apparently they are open late today because of the waves. Lots of patients complaining of seasickness." She pointed behind me. "Take those elevators to the bottom floor. Follow the hall around to the right. You'll see a red cross over the door."

I nodded. "Thank you."

I took the elevators to the bowels of the ship. It was much different from the fun and colorful atmosphere found on the upper decks. The hallway was painted hospital-white and lit by single bulbs spread out every few feet. The line of groaning people waiting to see the doctor wrapped around the corridor. And if the line hadn't tipped me off, the smell of antiseptic and vomit would have. Most of the visitors clutched at their stomachs like they were going to puke. Or they already had. I kept my distance and waited my turn as I tried to figure out these crazy things going on in my life.

And why they were happening to me.

As I got closer to the entrance of the doctor's office, I heard machines beeping. The beeps sounded like the noises I faced every time I visited Mom at the hospital—the times I actually went into her room. A wave of guilt almost knocked me over with its force. She sat in a coma at the hospital, and I was concerned about what Marcus might think of my panties.

I was such a bad daughter. If I could find a way out of this mess and back to her, I would try to make things right.

When my name was called, a fat nurse led me into a tiny square exam room. She motioned for me to sit on a miniature exam table. A small stool was tucked under the table. A sink that wouldn't fit a grapefruit inside was tucked into a mini counter with tissues, cotton balls, and tongue depressors in glass jars. With the two of us in there, there wasn't much room for anything else. I'd hoped the doctor didn't come in while the nurse was still with me. Someone would end up on my shaking lap.

She took my blood pressure, temperature, and pulse, and then asked why I was there. The shaking increased as I wondered if I should tell her how I'd just lost my mind.

"It's a personal matter," I replied. The fewer people that thought I was crazy, the better.

She left quickly and shut the door behind her with a frown on her chubby face. Two minutes later, a young woman walked in holding a clipboard. "Hello. I'm Dr. Hardy. What can I help you with today?"

I looked her up and down. She looked kind of familiar with long, dark red hair, intelligent green eyes, and a sprinkling of freckles across her nose. Without any makeup, she was pretty in a studious way. She didn't look old enough to be a doctor, but her lab coat said "Doctor" on it. A stethoscope hung around her slender neck like a medal, and pens poked out of her pocket.

I pursed my lips and reconsidered talking to this chick.

She sighed. "Honey, I've heard it all. Please, just tell me what's bothering you. I want to help, but we have a lot of people waiting and you need to talk to me."

The minute she spoke, I knew her voice. Then it hit me—she was the woman the day we departed, asking if I was okay.

I shrugged. "Okay, fine. But don't laugh."

"I won't laugh."

"Um..." I looked down at my hands. "I, uh, think I might be going crazy."

She put the clipboard on the micro-counter and stepped closer to me. "I'm listening."

I told her about my parents, Jessica, Joey, and Marcus. How everyone played a different role in my life on the ship than in my life at home. Dr. Hardy listened to me without prompting me to hurry, but most importantly without laughing.

She glanced at the door and suddenly looked like she didn't want to be in the room with me. "Miss Taylor, I'm afraid I can't help you yet."

I raised an eyebrow. "Yet? What does that mean?"

She laughed. "Sorry, dear, you misheard me. I said I can't let you fret. You'll be fine."

I frowned. "No, you didn't. I heard you. You said you can't help me *yet*. I might be going nuts, but there's nothing wrong with my hearing."

She grabbed the clipboard and reached out for the doorknob. "I have a lot of patients waiting, so I'll send the nurse back in to give you a shot for the seasickness. I hope you feel better."

"Wait," I called out, but she was already gone.

I hopped off the table. Screw this place. What kind of doctor was she? She didn't even listen to my real problem. Seasick? Please. Obviously she couldn't handle mental patients.

The nurse opened the door with a needle in hand. "I'm here for your—"

I put my hand up as I walked out. "Save it for someone who needs it."

When I left the office, I decided the only thing that could erase this craziness was sleep. At least in dreams, I knew things were supposed to be messed up. Maybe when I woke up everything would be back to normal. I went back to our cabin and let the darkness overtake me as fast as it would.

Cold air biting at my ass cheeks woke me the next morning. During the night, I had thrown the covers to the floor. The air conditioning vent now washed a cool breeze over me, and my panties and cami did nothing to stave off the wind. I grabbed the blanket off the floor and covered myself.

I peeked around the room for any evidence that I'd lost my mind the day before. Jessica slept on the couch on her back. Her right hand rested on a thin, flat stomach.

Thank God. The nightmare was over. My lips spread into an involuntary smirk. Ha! Autumn Rayne: 1, Psychotic Mental Breakdown: 0. A new day was starting, and it looked to be a good one.

I got up and stretched away the stress from yesterday. I looked down and noticed a blue piece of paper on the floor by the door. Ugh. It was probably from Marcus apologizing about last night. I walked over and picked it up. The neat handwriting looked familiar, but it wasn't Marcus's.

Joey. I thought he didn't know me yesterday?

I opened the note and read the printed words.

Dear Autumn,

I'm so glad we came on this trip together. Two wonderful years with you is more than anything I ever dreamt possible. It's been the ride of a lifetime. I hope we can look back on this cruise as the best vacation ever.

Love you more than life,

Joey

The note slipped from my fingers and drifted down to the floor like a fluffy snowflake.

Oh damn. What about Marcus? And Joey not knowing me? Or our usual game of shadower and shadow-ee?

I walked over to Jessica and shook her bare shoulder. Her golden hair was a tangled mess in her face. Last night's makeup left black tracks around her eyes, giving her the look of a raccoon.

"Jessica, you going to breakfast?" I whispered.

She didn't open her eyes but shook her head no. "If you see Marcus, tell him I'm sleeping in."

"Marcus? Why?"

She cracked a sleepy eye open. "So he can eat without me, silly. We all had a late night last night, but I'm sure he's hungry. He eats like a moose."

How did she know this about him? They only went on one date back home. Unless…

"Jessica, um, how do you know he eats like a moose? Have you seen him eat?"

She rolled her eye and closed it. "If I don't know how much he eats after eight months of dating, I should be shot. Now let me get some sleep. I'm tired. Go away."

She shooed me away with her slightly tanned hand.

Damn. Jessica and Marcus? I wondered if he acted like a sex-starved maniac with her like he did with me. "Okay, I'll be at the buffet."

She nodded and rolled over. For a second, I thought I spotted a tattoo on her shoulder, but that would never happen. She was totally against anything that permanently altered her perfect body. I tugged the blanket to sneak a peek, but she held it tight around herself as she slept.

I changed into a pale yellow sundress and went to the elevators. When I got off at the buffet, I saw Marcus and his parents standing in line. I didn't know if I should say anything, so I walked by and glanced at them. His parents ignored me but Marcus caught my eye. He winked at me and smirked.

I looked away quickly, unsure of what his gesture meant, and continued into the dining room.

Joey waited for me at the entrance to the food line in jeans shorts and a NY Giants jersey. He had two trays, with orange juice and a bowl of fresh fruit on each one.

"Good morning, Autumn. I hope you slept well. Hungry?" He kissed me on the cheek.

I pressed my hand to my cheek where he'd kissed me, and nodded. Oh God. What was I getting into today? Joey's warm kiss affected me more than I was willing to admit out loud.

"Good. Come on. I got our trays ready."

We went through the line and picked out our food. Joey stopped to wait for me as I buttered my toast. He reached with his long arms around the indecisive person in front of us to grab me a cheese Danish. I wondered if he would be sweet like that in real life. Or back home, if this was real and that wasn't. I had no idea anymore about anything. I couldn't even make my thoughts make sense.

We found an unoccupied table near the window and sat down. Joey took my tray from me and set it down so I could sit and pull in my chair.

How on earth could Marcus and Joey be related? I shook my head as I recalled how different things were yesterday.

"Are you enjoying the cruise so far?" he asked.

"Uh, yeah. It's been one surprise after another." That was an understatement.

He puffed out his chest and mimicked a superhero. "Well, you know me. Mr. Romantic." He looked me over, but not with the sex-crazed look Marcus had used. "You look pretty this morning. I hope you got some sleep after all our midnight madness last night. That color looks fantastic on you, by the way."

Midnight madness? Wasn't that some sports thing? "Um, thanks." We ate in near silence for a while. He refilled my OJ twice and got me another fork when mine fell on the floor.

"Did you see the island?" Joey pointed to a window across from us.

"No. I just see water and sky." I turned toward the window, filling my vision with the shades of blues outside. I swung around in my seat and nearly choked on my potatoes.

While the view from my window showcased the beautiful ocean and empty sea, the opposite window, facing the island, was full of wonder. Rows of colorful houses in hues of pink, blue, purple, and green dotted the landscape. Deep green leaves wrapped around giant fuchsia flowers. Palm trees swayed to the song of the breeze. Cruise ship passengers unloaded onto the docks wearing straw hats and carrying colorful totes. The bright morning sun cast a movie-star glow over everything it touched.

I turned back to Joey and smiled. "I've never seen anything so beautiful."

He reached across the table and caressed my cheek. "That's because you aren't looking at you." He dropped his hand from my face and grinned. "I'm taking you sightseeing after we eat. Whatever you want to do and see, just name it. The day is yours. But you might want to put on some sneakers in case we do a lot of walking."

Geez, no wonder the guy got stepped on at work all the time and stuck with the late shifts. He was so willing to bend over backwards for me. I'd heard he did that for his family, too.

Must be exhausting to take care of everyone else. Sadly, I'd never tried.

I shied away from his warm finger. No guy had ever been as gentle with me, and he didn't push like Marcus did. Marcus acted like hormones were more important to him than air. Joey acted like a hopeless romantic. Wasn't there anything in between?

As long as things with him stayed platonic like this, I could play along. I hadn't realized before now how safe he made me feel. Despite his annoying habit of always being right behind me, when he wasn't around I'd noticed his absence.

It was like he was growing on me. How could that be?

The sudden realization that Joey might be good boyfriend material caused a tightness in my chest and choked off my breath. Jessica had been saying it for months, but I had thought she just wanted to get me out of the house more. "Joey, I have to run to the bathroom. Be right back?"

"Sure. Take your time."

I put my napkin on the table and walked toward the ladies' room, shaking my head. I needed a shrink.

I turned the corner and yelped when someone grabbed me around the waist and pulled me into a hallway near the bathroom.

"Hey, get the hell off me!" I struggled to turn around to see who the hell was attempting to kidnap me.

"Shh, Raynie, it's just me," Marcus whispered in my ear. "I need a favor. Keep Jessica out of the buffet this morning for me, okay?"

I pushed hard against his chest. He released me. "Why? What are you up to, Marcus?" And why was he hiding from Jessica? After spending the last two days with him, I didn't trust him, but this sounded extra suspicious.

He dropped his hands to his sides and masked his face in innocence. "Nothing. Just a surprise for her, and I don't want her to see it until I'm ready." When he glanced around with shifty eyes, any part of me that might have believed him jumped ship.

I narrowed my eyes. "Yeah, sure. Like I believe that? You must think I'm an idiot."

He threw his head back and laughed. "You're good to your sister, Autumn. I can respect that. Just, please? It's nothing bad, I promise."

As he said that, his darting eyes stopped on someone behind me. His cheeks flushed the slightest bit, but it was enough.

I turned around. Olivia stood near the entrance to the buffet, trying to look like she wasn't listening to us.

Oh, shit. It hit me hard and fast—Marcus was cheating on Jessica with Olivia.

What a freakin' douchebag. But not in the least bit surprising.

No way. I'd never let him get away with this. Jessica didn't deserve that. I never cheated, no matter how much I wanted out of a relationship. Jessica didn't, either. We both felt it was the lowest thing someone could do to another person.

And if Marcus thought I was going to let this go, he had another thing coming. "Marcus, if you think you're going to cheat on Jessica and I'm going to cover for you, you'd better think again."

He laughed in my ear. "Give me a break, Rayne. I'm not cheating on Jessica! Why would I do that right here on the ship, in front of you guys? Really, give me some credit."

He did have a point, though my suspicions clung to me like cat hair on a hoodie.

I checked back over my shoulder. Olivia was gone. Okay, so maybe I was just going nuts on this cruise through Hell and imagined her. I'd give him the benefit of the doubt.

For now.

"Fine, whatever, Marcus. But I'm keeping my eye on you. You'd better be good to Jessica. Speaking of which, she said to tell you she's sleeping in and to go ahead and eat."

He flashed his amazing smile and pulled me into a hug. "Thanks, babe. I knew you'd help me out."

A girl walking by in flip-flops stopped dead in her tracks to stare. How rude. This did not concern her.

I followed the flip-flops up and over a skin-tight outfit and looked right into Olivia's angry eyes. With the shock she didn't try to hide evident on her face, I assumed that, today, she knew me.

And today she looked pissed off. She put her hands on her hips. "What the hell are you doing, Autumn? Isn't that mechanic guy your boyfriend? You're even trashier than I thought." She tossed her bouncy dark curls and sneered at me, a calculating look on her smug face. "But this could be worth something to me."

"Nothing's going on here, Olivia." I said her name like it hurt my mouth to utter such a terrible thing. "Marcus and I are just talking."

She stayed put, tapping her polished nail on her front tooth. "Yeah, sure. Doubt that. I know you, and I know Marcus."

Marcus loosened his grip on me and looked over his shoulder at her. "Take a hike, chick. And keep your mouth shut around Joey. You didn't see a thing."

I pushed against his chest again. "Marcus, you're making it sound like something's going on here! It's not." I focused on Olivia. "So go ahead and tell Joey anything you want. It'll be bullshit."

Marcus let go of me and straightened up, then turned and sauntered off with such confidence that I wanted to beat it out of him. He stopped about twenty feet away and called back over his shoulder. "Tell your sister I'll see her later."

When I looked back at Olivia, she was glaring. "How can you cheat on that sweet guy? Don't you have any conscience at all?"

I jabbed my finger in her face. "Like you can talk? You're such a hypocrite! You want to talk about conscience when you blackmailed me? And I already told you, nothing is going on with Marcus. So just drop the little shocked act and leave me alone."

"I have better things to do than stand here with you, anyway." She spun around, then stopped. "But I might find Joey first, and have a nice little chat with him." She stalked toward the buffet.

I rushed after her. When I caught up, I tugged on her arm. "Knock yourself out. I'm so sure he'll take your word over mine."

I turned and stomped away, hoping she would come after me. At this point, I was not above hitting her.

I ran back into the restaurant without going to the bathroom. Olivia didn't follow. Joey smiled up at me when I approached our table.

"Everything okay? You look flushed. Sit down."

He reached up and gently pulled me down next to him. The love in his eyes was so obvious, it made me want to cry. If Olivia told him I was cheating on him, he would be devastated. I couldn't imagine causing him that kind of pain. He didn't deserve it.

Tears welled up in my eyes. None of this was good. And with Olivia prowling around, ready to get something out of my misery, I'd had enough.

Joey reached over and stroked my cheek. "What's wrong, sweetie? Why are you crying?"

What was I supposed to tell him? I didn't even know what to say. My emotions ran around my body like a runaway rollercoaster that had fallen off the track. "I have to run back to the room. I'll be back, okay? Just give me a few minutes. I…I think I'm a little seasick."

He nodded and pursed his lips.

I got up, left everything on the table, and ran all the way to the cabin. I was out of breath by the time I made it to my door. I inserted my key but the door swung open, ripping the key from my shaking hand. Jessica stood in front of me with her hands on her hips, her pajamas still on.

"Where the hell have you been?" she demanded. "You don't leave me a note, you just take off and I wake up here alone? What the hell, Autumn?"

I just stared at her. "Cut the crap, Jessica. I'm not in the mood." I pushed past her and walked into the room.

She closed the door behind me and turned to glare. "Well?"

"Well what? I went to breakfast with Joey. I even asked if you were going and you shook your head no. I told you I was going."

"You did not ask. I would've woken up."

"Jessica, you were lying on the couch, your makeup smeared, hair in your face, and I woke you up. You even said to tell Marcus to eat without you because you'd had a late night. So leave me alone. It's not my fault you were talking in your sleep when I woke you."

She turned down the glare and dropped her hands. "Fine. Sorry, I was just worried about you." She pulled off her pajamas and sifted through a drawer full of her clothes.

No tats. Geez, my mind was taking a walk off the plank for sure.

"So did you have a nice breakfast with Joey?"

"Um, yeah. He's still there. I ran back here to ask you for Dad's cell phone number."

She gave me a puzzled look. "Uncle Dan's cell phone?"

I shook my head. "Not Dan. Dad. I need Dad's number. I must have deleted it from my phone. Can you give it to me?"

Her face turned pink, then red, then purple. Tears welled in her eyes, then ran over, adding to the mascara mess. She wiped an escaped tear with the back of her hand. "Autumn Rayne, how could you…please go. Now. I can't handle this." She slumped down on the couch and covered her face. She pointed to the door with a thin, unsteady finger.

I sat next to her. "Jessica, what is your problem? You told me yesterday to try his cell and I forgot to get the number from you. Why are you freaking out now?"

She pushed me away from her. "Stop it. Right now. Please, Autumn. Don't do this to me."

I sighed. "Jessica, look. I'm just trying to make sense of things and I'm having a really hard time understanding what's going on. Why are you crying? Tell me, dammit!"

"I can't…I…" She reached for a tissue and wiped her face.

I grabbed my churning stomach and bent over. My breaths came quick and ragged. Did I hope? Not hope? My brain fought over living and dead images of both parents. Caskets, hugs, hospitals, and smiles all tried to win me over.

"Jessica? Where's Dad?"

She narrowed her eyes at me. Her tears slowed. "Mom and Dad have been gone for over ten years. Give me one good reason why I would tell you to call him on his cell!"

I crossed my arms over my chest, grasping at the shred of hope I had left. Maybe in this changed reality, he really was dead. "Define…define gone."

She widened her eyes. "Dead, Autumn! Killed in that awful car wreck! What is the matter with you? When Aunt Christine paid for this trip so you could be with Joey, she sent me along with Marcus, hoping you and I could get closer. Obviously that's not happening. You're still a spoiled rotten child hell-bent on making me miserable. Go back to Joey. I'm sure he's waiting for you."

I stared at the floor for a second, then got up. I went to reach for the door handle when she called out to me.

I didn't turn around. "Yeah?"

"When we get back to Jersey, you're moving out."

I faced her and crossed my arms over my chest. She couldn't be serious. "What?"

Jessica scowled at me. "You heard me. You quit school, you fight me on everything, and now this with Mom and Dad?" She wiped her nose with the tissue. "I just can't handle it, Autumn. I think it's time for you to go somewhere to get the guidance you need, that I obviously can't give you. I'm sure Joey plans on living with you now, which is fine, but you could benefit from some professional help."

I stood frozen to my spot, my brain and body unable to function. Jessica was kicking me out? Where was I supposed to go? I wasn't ready yet.

"Jessica, what are you talking about?"

She shook her head. The sadness in her eyes showed me she wasn't doing this to be mean, but because she thought it was best for me. "The only reasons I haven't done this sooner are Emmie and Joey. I hate for this to affect them, too, but you leave me no choice."

"Who the hell is Emmie? "

"Very funny. This is what I mean. You can't even take me seriously when your entire family is at stake."

What the hell was she talking about? "Jessica, you and Mom are my family."

"No. We used to be a family. Now it's just you and me, and you're ruining that, too. I can't handle you anymore."

My eyes widened. "That's nice! What, am I supposed to be some orphan now? You and my life back home is all I know!"

Her lip quivered. "Before we left for the cruise, I looked into some places for troubled girls. Don't worry, they're all in the area so I can visit you often. But I'm not sure about that now, with everything that happened with Joey last night. And—"

I held up both hands. I'd heard enough of her bullshit. "You know what, Jessica? Fuck off. The minute we land, or whatever the hell this ship does, I'm gone. You don't need to worry about me anymore. I'm going to the island with Joey. You can kiss my ass."

I ripped off my sundress and threw on a pair of jeans shorts and a black T-shirt that said "cloudy with a chance of sarcasm" on it. The entire time, Jessica sat on the couch and stared at her hands.

Whatever. I was so done with her, just like everyone else.

Once I tied my sneakers nice and tight, I left the room with my beach bag slung low and my blood pressure sky-high. Joey met me at the gangway. His electric smile set off his tan skin, making his face glow. A stuffed red backpack clung to his well-defined back. A smile formed on my lips despite the daggers Jessica had just thrown into my heart.

"Hey." I walked up to him.

He leaned down and kissed me on the cheek, lingering for a few seconds with his warm lips on my skin. They were disconcertingly soft. His clean-shaven face was smooth against mine. "Ready for some fun? I have a nice surprise for you!"

I sucked in a deep breath and sighed. The distraction was just the thing I needed after Jessica basically told me she was throwing me out. "Sure."

He lifted my chin with his finger. "Hey, everything okay?"

I shook my head. "I just had a fight with Jessica. She's kicking me out when we get back to New Jersey."

His eyes went wide. "Are you serious? I mean, do you think she'll really do it? She isn't that type of person."

I shrugged. "Apparently she is, and to answer your question, yes, I think she'll do it. It sounded real enough when she talked about it." I tried to come across as blasé about the whole thing, despite my fear that she would do it.

He folded me into his arms. "Don't worry, Autumn. We'll work it out. She's just upset, but everything will be fine. I won't let anything happen to you, okay? Besides, I figured we would move in together when we got back, so it doesn't really matter. Don't you want to do that?"

I stiffened. Live with him? At my age? There was no way I was moving in with him or anyone else in Jersey.

And if Jessica kicked me out, it would be the last she'd ever see of me.

I sighed. "Let's not talk about this anymore. It's ruining my day."

"No problem. Let's go."

He took my hand and led me through security, releasing it only when he had to insert our cabin keycards into the ID system. We walked down the gangway and stepped onto the wooden dock.

Toasted air lapped at my exposed skin. Somewhere off in the distance, steel drums played a calypso beat. The colors I'd witnessed through the window seemed to have suddenly become HD. Spread out in front of us was the most beautiful place I'd ever seen.

The sun warmed the coconut-scented breeze that made the palm trees dance. A cloudless sky negated the saying on my shirt. The pastel-colored cottages now resembled rainbow sherbet. The ocean supporting our ship was crystal-clear and smooth as glass. I closed my eyes and paused, imprinting this memory on my brain. The smells, the sounds, the sensations—I opened myself up like a sponge to absorb it all.

Joey wrapped his arm around my waist. "Hungry? I'm taking you out to lunch."

I looked up into his eyes. I wanted to keep him at a distance, but the newness of this side of Joey and his genuine happiness melted the ice wall I'd formed to shut him out.

I decided to forget about Jessica for now and enjoy the day. For all I knew, it could be my last. "Where?"

"It's a surprise." He reached around to the back of his pack and pulled out a slip of paper. "Got a map to a nice park nearby, too. Do you need anything before we go?"

"Um, chocolate," I said. "Oh, and I heard this island has pink sand. Can we look for some?"

"Sure. Let's get to the park. We can sit and eat, then check out the beach, okay?" He patted the backpack and winked at me. "Got the chocolate covered—M&M's. No worries about melting in this tropical heat."

Geez, he really had thought of everything.

I nodded and gestured for him to lead. He slid his hand into mine and led me a few blocks from the dock to a hidden park entrance. As we walked, we passed more colorful houses, local cops in Bermuda shorts, and couples being pulled around in horse-drawn carriages. The park didn't look like much until we entered the grounds, but once inside, the nearly deserted place felt magical.

Deep-green foliage surrounded bright white, pink, and red flowers. Wooden benches were tucked under huge trees. Birdsongs rang through the air. A round stone gate at the far corner of the park reminded me of something out of Hobbiton. It resembled a fat, inverted horseshoe overgrown with vibrant green vines. Tiny multicolored flowers dotted the vines like Christmas ornaments.

I kicked off my flip-flops and let the strange grass taste my feet. The cool blades sucked the worry out of my warm feet and drained away my anxiety about the cruise and my life. I closed my eyes and breathed in a giant breath.

"Do you like it?" Joey asked.

"I love it. It's the most amazing place I've ever seen. How did you find it?"

He winked at me. "It's a secret. Come on. See that gate over there?" He pointed to the Hobbit gate. "It's called a Moongate. There's a legend that says people who walk through one have good luck. Want to give it a try?"

I nodded, dropped my beach bag, and made a beeline for the bringer of luck. When Joey started to follow, I put a hand up to stop him. "Um, do you mind if I go through it first? Maybe we will get twice the luck if we each go through separately." I wanted to do this alone. I needed more luck than fifty trips through the gate could offer, and I didn't want to risk him soaking up some of mine, selfish as that sounded.

He stopped and motioned for me to continue.

My pulse raced as I approached the flower-covered gate. I didn't know why, but something seemed to be pulling me, beckoning me to get through the gate right this second. I paused at the mouth of the giant ring and peeked through.

On the other side, an expanse of bright green grass ended at the choppy ocean a mile into the distance. Several wooden benches lined a shady area to my left. Three long tables with a brunch buffet stood off to the right, and tables and chairs were set up near the food. About twenty people dressed in summer clothes milled about. Soft music played from speakers set at the edge of one of the buffet tables.

Assuming I'd almost crashed someone's party, I turned to go.

"Autumn, honey," a familiar female voice said from behind me. "Surprise! Come on in, don't be shy."

I spun back around and searched for the source of the voice. Joey came up from behind and slid his arms around my waist. "Isn't this great?"

The woman who'd called me walked closer. I squinted to see who she was, but in the bright Bermuda sun, I could only make out the shape of a person. She stepped into the shade of a giant palm tree, making her features visible. My knees wobbled and my breath caught in my chest. Thankfully, Joey's arms around me held me up. "Mom?" I whispered.

Joey chuckled in my ear. "No, sweetie. It's Aunt Christine. And look who she brought with her." He pointed at my aunt's arms, which held a moving bundle in a blanket.

Aunt Christine's tanned skin glowed against her white cotton summer dress, her light brown hair piled in loose curls on top of her head. Her warm brown eyes matched the shade of my mom's eyes. People always said they could be twins.

Today, I believed it.

I offered a weak smile when she stopped in front of me. I didn't know if my legs would continue to hold me up, but they worked so far. "Aunt Christine! Wow! What are you doing here?"

She glanced at Joey and smiled.

"I asked her to come to the island for the days our ship was in port. I knew you would miss her and would be thrilled to see them." He squeezed my middle and kissed my neck.

"Them?" I asked. "Who else is here?"

The blanket in her arms moved again. I hooked a finger around the edge to peek inside. "What do you have in there, a puppy?"

Joey and Aunt Christine laughed. Then, from the edge of the blanket, a tiny pink face peeked out, looked at me, and smiled.

My mouth dropped to my knees. The moment froze in time. I could see what everyone around me was doing in slow motion. Aunt Christine bounced the baby up and down. Joey stroked my hair and spoke to me, but I had no idea what he was saying. The other people ate, drank, swayed to the music, and laughed like they didn't have a care in the world.

This child was my clone. Her face was a miniature version of mine, with eyes like…

"Mommy's here, Emmie! Say 'hi,'" Aunt Christine said, making the baby wave with her pudgy hand. At me.

"Um, Aunt Christine, where's her mother?" I mean, she couldn't possibly mean me. The kid looked like me, but still.

Aunt Christine and Joey laughed. "Silly Mommy." Joey nudged my shoulder with his. "That's not how you play peek-a-boo."

Shock and fear crawled up my spine. This baby was mine?

I had a freakin' baby?

I had no idea what her name was. I had no idea who the father was supposed to be. I had no idea what to do. I couldn't take care of myself, so how was I supposed to take care of a tiny person? Thank God Aunt Christine had her, because that was exactly where she was staying.

With someone who could handle the baby thing.

And, oh, my God, suddenly what Jessica had said this morning made sense. Emmie and Joey were my family now. And when Joey had said find a place for the *three* of us, I thought maybe he meant me, him, and his mother.

I was so wrong.

"I'm so glad Joey thought of this. Where's your sister?" Aunt Christine asked.

"Uh…Jessica?"

She pulled the rumpled blanket off the squirming baby and chuckled. "Yes, unless you have another sister that I'm unaware of."

Well, with the way things were going, I guess that was possible. "Um, she's coming."

Here in the Triangle, many impossible things seemed possible. The evidence? The baby in front of me when I'd yet to have sex. I had come close, and had no problem fooling around, but I didn't plan on giving all of me up until I was completely ready.

I had yet to be ready.

I looked down at my stomach. Smooth and flat. I lifted the edge of my shirt to check for stretch marks or some other hint that this baby had come from me. Nothing.

The baby, now peeled from her cocoon, reached for me. "Ga, ga, ga," she babbled in a little baby voice.

I got that everything I was going through didn't make sense, but each thing that changed caught me off guard. It was like waking up each day as a different person. I had to get used to who I was before I could function as the person du jour.

Automatically, my hands reached out to take her. She lunged at me without hesitation and hugged my neck with surprising force for such a tiny thing.

"Uh, hi, sweetheart. Are you having fun with Aunt Christine?"

She ignored my question and wrapped her fingers around my hair. Her wide, brown eyes took in the sights all around us.

I'd seen those dark brown eyes before.

Oh, shit on a shingle.

Joey came around to stand in front of me and rubbed the baby's back. "Happy to see Mommy, Emmie? I knew she would love this surprise!" His eyes beamed as he held my gaze.

She squealed and reached for him.

"Hiya, Emmie Wemmie!" He tickled her chin and grinned. "Want to come to Daddy?"

That was it. My arms went limp and down the baby went. Joey snatched her tiny body before she hit the ground, thank God. My knees gave out and before I realized what was happening, my butt smacked into the grassy hill.

"Autumn! Are you all right?" He handed the baby to Aunt Christine and knelt beside me, lifting my head into his lap. I gulped in some air and slammed my eyes shut for a second.

"Autumn, honey!" Aunt Christine said, clutching the baby to her chest. "What's the matter? Holy crap, you almost dropped the baby!" The panic in her eyes increased my own. What would have happened to that child if I'd dropped her on her head?

I rubbed my eyes and tried to stop the spinning in my brain. "I'm fine, Joey. Thanks. I think…I think the sun is getting to me. Is Emmie all right?" He helped me stand and held me as I tested my ability to remain upright.

"She's fine. Joey caught her just in time." Aunt Christine tickled Emmie's chin. "Daddy's the best, isn't he?"

Joey kept his grasp on me. "You sure you're okay?"

I nodded. "I'm good. Yeah. I'll be okay. Thanks."

"Come on. Maybe some food will help." Aunt Christine walked us over to the buffet and helped me fill my plate with exotic fruit, fresh vegetables, and grilled chicken and shrimp, all the while bouncing Emmie on her hip.

I would never be able to do that. I wasn't even a real mother and I had already failed at motherhood.

"What's going on?" I asked.

"A luncheon set up by a local pub. Don't worry, I already paid for all of our meals. Help yourself to anything." She picked up a celery stick off my plate and chomped down. "Want me to take Emmie while you and Joey eat? Or do you miss the little chubber too much to part with her now?"

I looked at the baby in her arms. I couldn't even tell how old she was, because I knew nothing about babies. "Um, please hold her for me. It'll, um, make eating easier. Thanks a lot."

Aunt Christine smiled and cooed, and Emmie did the same. At least they seemed to like each other.

"Autumn, there's an empty table over there." Joey took my plate and led me to the table. When I sat down, he set the food in front of us. "I'll go get us some drinks."

Joey headed to the drink table with confidence in his stride. He stopped where Aunt Christine and Emmie were playing on the grass and squeezed the little girl's cheek. She beamed at him, kicking her little feet and reaching out to him. He leaned down and kissed her head before getting us two glasses of Coke and returning to the table.

"I can't believe Emmie's six months old already. Where does the time go?" He shook his head as he watched my aunt blow bubbles at the baby. "So, good surprise?"

I forced my best smile out. "Yes, thank you, Joey. The best. How did you set this up?"

"When we planned the trip, I called Christine about meeting us since she would be watching the baby. She thought it was a great idea, so here she is. But she's only staying on the island for two nights. I knew you would miss Emmie, so this worked out perfectly."

I stared at him. His face held the contentment of a kitten full of warm milk. Since he was Emmie's father, I guess we'd already…

The thought of Joey and me sleeping together set my face on fire. Holy shit.

And here I was blaming Marcus for being the horndog.

My eyes flashed down to his crotch, which only increased the redness filling up my cheeks.

He glanced at me and frowned. "You okay? You're all flushed. I guess the heat really is getting to you." He placed his hand on my forehead.

I nodded. "I'm fine. Thanks for asking." His expression relaxed, and he resumed munching.

I focused on the baby, trying to see a resemblance to him. As I stared at her sweet face, his features came into sharp focus. The dark eyes, the dark hair, the same chin.

Joey was my baby's father.

The food I'd eaten wanted to come back up. "Joey, I think I ate too much. I'm gonna lie back on the grass and close my eyes for a few, okay?"

He stroked my cheek. "Sure, baby. I'll keep an eye on things."

I found a soft patch of grass under a huge tree and reclined. Within minutes, I let the sleep take me away from what was the strangest vacation of my life.

"Autumn? You okay?"

I opened my eyes to see Joey's face inches from mine. Concern crossed his features.

I blinked a few times. The sun had changed position, but I had no idea what time it was. Most of the people who had been in the park were gone, and I glanced around but didn't see Aunt Christine or Emmie. I leaned forward to get up and grabbed my head. "Whoa, head rush. I need to get back to the ship."

"Sure, sweetie. Come on, I'll grab your bag."

"Where'd everyone go?"

He chuckled as he helped me up and brushed the dirt off my butt. "Emmie got cranky, so Christine took her back to the hotel. I told her we'd check in later."

Ugh, I didn't know what to do now. Wouldn't I seem like a terrible mother if I didn't ask to see the kid some more? Then again, I had never been a mother, so what did I know? "Okay. As long as she's being, um, taken care of, I guess I'm ready to go." We headed back to the ship, my mind reeling as I tried to figure out just what was going on.

When we got back to my room, I wasn't sure what I wanted to do, but Joey deserved a little love for setting up such a great surprise. "Thank you for today, and for thinking of that. Bringing them here…it was just amazing. No one has ever done anything like that for me." As I spoke the words, I realized how true they were. His answering smile showed off his happiness.

"You're welcome. You would have done…oh, wait. I have something else for you." He turned and reached into his backpack. "I thought you might want this, so you won't miss her too much." Joey handed me what I assumed was one of Emmie's stuffed bears. "I'll be right back," he said as he deposited me on the bed and went to find his grandparents to let them know we had gotten back okay.

Sitting alone on my bed, I stared at the wall as I wondered what it would really be like to be a teen mom. I didn't know anyone yet who'd had a kid, and none of my cousins were babies, so this was totally foreign territory. My eyes found the bear sitting on the counter by the door. I hoped the baby would stay with Christine on the island, because there was no way I could fake taking care of her.

Joey must've hunted down Jessica for me because she ran into the room, slamming the door behind her.

"Autumn, what happened? Joey said something happened to you in the park." She knelt in front of me and took my hands in hers.

I stared at her, the words in my brain failing to make their way to my mouth.

She shook my hands. "Speak, Autumn! What happened?"

"I just…I just…um, I fell asleep in the park. I have a headache."

She gave my hands back to me and stood up. "That's it? A headache? You leave the baby with Aunt Christine and run back to the cabin for a damn headache?" She threw herself down on the couch. "You need to grow up, Autumn. You're a mother now. Put your kid first and stop acting like a baby yourself."

I sighed and stood up. "Jessica, I'm not trying to upset you. I didn't know Joey went looking for you. I'm okay. I probably just got too much sun." I touched her back, but she ignored me.

"Where's Emmie now?"

"Aunt Christine took her back to the hotel when I fell asleep."

Jessica threw her hands up in the air. "That's nice. Way to take care of your child. Just dump her off on Aunt Christine. As usual."

"Oh, yeah? Well then, what about you? Huh? You just told me this morning you were kicking me out. Way to take care of me, right?" My hands shook as I realized it wasn't just me she didn't want anymore. "And what about Emmie? Does she get to go to this group home place, too? Where God knows what could happen to her?" I sucked in a breath. "You know what? It doesn't matter, because we'll be moving in with Joey when we get back anyway. Emmie will be just fine with us."

She refused to look at me. "No, she won't, Autumn. I planned on adopting her. You guys are too young to care for a baby. You can't even take care of yourself."

WTF? "So you're kicking me out AND taking my kid away? You know what? I don't need this shit from you. Screw you. I'll leave you alone. Sorry to have bothered you." I walked out the door and stomped down the hall toward the elevators. I hopped on to head toward the buffet for a drink. When the doors slid open, Marcus was standing nearby—with Olivia's hand on his ass. Classy.

He grinned at me and cornered me against the wall. "Keep your mouth shut about Olivia, Autumn. If you say one word to Jessica, you'll be sorry."

"Stop it!" I shoved hard against his chest. Marcus and his pressure was the last thing I needed right now. He didn't let up.

I pushed harder. "If Joey sees this he's going to be pissed. Get off!"

"What the hell is going on here?" Joey said, storming toward us.

I snapped my head around to face Joey. Marcus released me, smirked, and took off down the hall.

"Joey, he just threatened me!" I pointed a shaking finger at Marcus's retreating figure.

Joey looked down at me, anger growing in his eyes. "What did he say?"

I grabbed Joey's hand and squeezed. "He's cheating on Jessica. I just saw him with a girl I know from high school. He told me I'd be sorry if I opened my mouth."

His jaw tightened. "He's so not getting away with that. Where did he go?" His brown eyes darkened as he spoke, and his biceps flexed under his shirt as he scanned the hall for Marcus.

Oh boy. I didn't want Joey to get arrested because of me. Or thrown in ship jail.

"I don't know, and I don't care. I can take care of it myself. You should know that."

"Autumn, he's going to answer to me whether you tell me where he is or not. No one threatens my wife and gets away with it."

I choked on my saliva. "What? I'm sorry, can you repeat that?"

His brown eyes focused on me with such intensity, I couldn't look away if I'd tried. "Autumn, part of my job as your husband is to protect you. And I take that very seriously."

My gaze snapped down to my ring finger. No rings were there, but a faint tan line proved that I'd had a ring on at some point.

He must have noticed me checking out my finger. "I'm sorry, baby. I figured we could choose our wedding rings when we get home since we got married on the spur of the moment. If you'd like, we could check out the jewelry store on the ship instead of waiting."

I got married? When the hell did I do that? *Why* the hell did I do that? I'm only seventeen! I shook my head, hoping it would clear this newest wave of weirdness out. "Not yet. I…I gotta go call Aunt Christine's hotel and check on the kid. Does she know about the wedding? I mean, does anyone?"

He shook his head. "We decided to keep it between us until we can afford a reception back home once you turn eighteen. So no, we haven't told anyone else. Only your sister and Marcus know. And your sister consented to the marriage, so we're good."

I turned to leave, but he grabbed my arm. "Autumn, wait. You know how much I love you, right?"

I nodded.

"And you know I'd do anything for you and Emmie. So, I don't want you to worry about Marcus. I'll take care of everything."

Days of confusion and disappointment and anger and shock built up inside of me. I sighed so long and loud I didn't think I had any breath left in me. "Joey, Jessica just told me that besides kicking me out, she plans on adopting Emmie." I stared at the ground, avoiding his eyes and the hurt I knew would be in them. "All I can say is, I'm really sorry."

I blinked several times to make the tears go away, but I couldn't hold it in any longer. The tears soaked my face, and the more I tried to wipe them away, the harder they fell. Joey scooped me into his long arms and carried me outside into the salty ocean air. He headed to a chair, then sat with me in his lap. I didn't have the strength to fight anymore. My guilt, anger, disappointment, and sadness leaked out of me with each tear that fell.

He stroked my hair and shushed me as I cried into his chest. His even heartbeat sang to my ear. "Don't worry, baby. We'll take care of it. I'll handle everything. She can't just take the baby from both of us."

Joey was turning out to be more decent than I'd expected. Maybe if he was able to look past all of my faults, I could do the same for him and his over-eager attempts to go out with me back home.

I sat up and wiped the tears from my face and hair. Joey stared at me with the most caring eyes I had ever seen. "I'm sorry, Joey. Look, let me go get my head on straight. I think I got too much sun or something. Can we meet for dinner?"

He smiled. "Sure. Promise me you'll come."

I took his hand. "I promise. I'll be there. Meet me at the buffet entrance at seven, okay?"

He squeezed my hand. "Sure thing. You're my life, Autumn Rayne. You and Emmie. Never forget that, okay?"

I nodded. The lump forming in my throat made it difficult to speak.

Jessica was reading a book on the couch when I walked into our cabin. She refused to look at me. I walked straight to her, sat down, and hugged her. "I'm sorry, Jessica. It's been a strange few days for me."

She sat rigidly.

I squeezed tighter. "Really. I'm really sorry. Please, don't be mad at me. I want to have fun on our trip. You can be mad at me back home, okay? I'll even let you lecture me." I offered a smile. "But please don't kick me out and take Emmie. I promise I'll do better."

She remained motionless for a moment, then let out a deep breath and hugged me back. "Aunt Christine is right. We should work hard to be good to each other, don't you think?"

"Yes. Let's try. I'm going to meet Joey for dinner. See you later?"

"Sure. After dinner I might go to a show, but I'll be back at some point. And Autumn? Be good to Joey. He's a really nice guy. And he treats Emmie like gold. He's a rare catch."

I was learning that. "I will. I promise."

She rubbed my arm. "Good. Now that you're married, I guess if things go okay, he can move into your bedroom."

My breath caught. How could I ask her about the wedding without sounding insane? "Um, Jessica…I forgot what you wore to the wedding. Do you still have that dress?"

She chuckled. "Of course. It's in the closet." She pointed to the closet behind me. "Why, did you want to borrow it?"

Why would she have the wedding dress here? Unless…

I glanced at the pile of magazines and activity sheets sitting on the table. On top of the pile, a picture of me, Joey, Jessica, and the captain of the ship stood out. I held a bouquet of flowers, and Joey held me.

Printed across the top were the words "Our Wedding." The date? Today.

"Um, Jessica," I said, grabbing the photo and staring at it. "When was this taken?"

She shook her head. "You really are getting too much sun. It followed the midnight buffet on the top deck by the pool. So, less than twenty-four hours ago? You'd think you'd remember your own wedding."

Yeah, you'd think.

I showered and slipped on a blue floral dress. When I got to the buffet, Joey was waiting for me with a box of chocolates. He looked great in khaki pants and a light orange shirt. I walked over to him and threw my arms around him. He hugged me back and held me tight.

The way my heart sped up surprised me. His warm body against mine made my spine tingle.

"I hope you like this kind of chocolate. It's all they had at the gift shop."

I opened the box, sniffed them, and nodded. "I'm so sorry. I had a talk with Jessica. She won't kick me out or try to take Emmie, as long as I get my shit together." Being able to do that was another matter, but still. I could try.

"I'm confident everything will be fine, babe." He took my hand and led me through the line, filling both of our plates with steak, baked potatoes, rolls, and salad. He helped me with everything, just like a gentleman from those old black and white movies.

I didn't think they existed anymore.

I tried to be inconspicuous as I glanced around to see if Marcus was in the dining room. I didn't see him anywhere. I breathed a sigh of relief and sat down with Joey at the table he chose. If he caught a glimpse of Marcus, things would likely get ugly.

Once we sat, he glanced around the room, and I would've bet anyone a million bucks he was searching for Marcus.

We munched on dinner as Joey talked about people I'd never met and recalled things we had never done together. But he was happy, and I was glad to not be fighting with anyone, so I just smiled a lot and nodded.

And it felt good. Why hadn't I allowed myself to feel good sooner? I was learning that, sometimes, life just sucked. And if this trip taught me anything, it was to go with the flow.

I was trying. Besides, did I have much choice? So much was out of my control. The only control I had was in the choices I made.

I needed to make better choices.

After dinner, Joey led me out of the dining room to the outside deck. I didn't ask him where we were going, but instead let him surprise me. The ocean was beautiful, and the night air warm and refreshing. I reached for the railing and looked over the side. The frothy waves crashed along the ship's edge. I closed my eyes and listened to the ship's engine hum a lullaby. It was the best I'd felt in days.

What if I got home and found this to be my permanent reality? For once, I thought it was something I could get used to.

Then I heard a baby cry off in the distance and changed my mind. I knew I wasn't ready to be a mom.

But being Joey's girl? Maybe.

He put his arms around me from behind and rested his chin on my head. I let myself enjoy the moment. It felt good to not be working so hard to push him away.

The breeze picked up and I shivered. He tightened his arms around me. "I know we're still young, Autumn, but I know this marriage will work. We both want it to. For us, and for Emmie."

I couldn't imagine a time or place where I would have said yes to his proposal except for on this screwed-up ship. I wasn't even eighteen yet. I had no plans for the future other than escaping from Jersey and starting over somewhere. Anywhere.

And now with Joey treating me like royalty, instead of the royal pain in the ass that I was, I didn't know how to act or think or feel. Maybe life wouldn't be so bad with a good guy to love me…

Ugh! No. I had to stop this right now. None of this was real. I repeated it to myself—none of this is real. I couldn't let a little fantasy change my whole life. I was getting ready for my life to begin. In another place. And another time. And now I had no idea what to do. As his warm arms held me with strength and love, I didn't want to keep pushing him away. I settled my head against his chest and sighed.

"How do you feel, babe?" He kissed the top of my head.

How did I feel? Confused. Scared. Upset. Nervous. Exhausted. And something else…

Oh yeah. I knew how I felt.

I felt like jumping off the boat.

Twelve

"I feel like getting some sleep," I said.

He looked at his feet and nodded. "Okay. Let's get to bed."

He wound his arm around my waist and led me through the pool deck to the elevators. He frowned as he pushed the button for down and waited.

Even though I'd done nothing wrong in reality, I felt guilty for some reason. Before the cruise, he annoyed me, but I was discovering some of the goodness in him as the cruise pushed on. Did I even deserve to be a part of his life?

And what did he mean, "Let's get to bed"? I hoped he didn't think we were going to sleep together. Married or not, I would not share his bed tonight.

That was just not happening.

The elevator doors opened. Marcus stepped out and looked at us. He started walking away, but Joey sneered at him.

That did it.

He changed course and walked up to Joey, jabbing a finger in his face. "Hey man, what's your problem?"

My mouth fell open and my nerves ignited. These two were about to have a major throw down, and I was the reason.

I grabbed Marcus's arm and shook him. "Marcus, you'd better leave before someone gets hurt."

He wasn't deterred. "Like I'm scared of him?" He jerked his thumb toward Joey. "You've got to be kidding." He flexed his biceps like that would somehow save him.

Wrong.

Joey dropped his arm from around my waist and balled his hands into fists. "Man, Autumn better have been kidding when she said you threatened her, because I know you can't be that stupid."

Marcus laughed with shimmering eyes and stepped closer to Joey. "What I say to Autumn has nothing to do with you, pal." His eyes didn't release Joey's as he said to me, "Besides, Rayne and I have a history together, don't we, Rayne?"

"No!" I snapped.

"Really? Remember right before you got pregnant with this grease monkey's baby, when you came to me about what to do? You weren't happy with him then." He smirked at Joey. "And you don't look happy now, either."

I stepped between them, bracing myself for the fight. Joey remained frozen.

"Don't listen to him, Joey. He's full of shit."

Joey defrosted and grabbed my shoulders, gently shoving me out of the way. He gave me a sad glance before leaning over Marcus and poking his shoulder. "Stay the hell away from her, understand? I will NOT warn you again," he said in a low growl. "Threaten her again, and it will be the end of you. I promise."

Marcus didn't back down. "Yeah, I'm so scared. See me shaking?" He motioned toward me with his eyes. "And since Rayne slept with me first, you just got my sloppy seconds."

Joey exploded into a fit of rage, shoving Marcus back against the wall. He pinned him there, with his elbow pressing on Marcus's neck. "You're one word away from death, little man. Go ahead and push me. Do it. I would love an excuse to end this."

Joey's aggression paralyzed me. I never knew he had it in him. I stared in horror as Marcus's face turned red, then purple, then blue. His eyes bulged.

"Joey! Marcus! Stop it!" Jessica yelled from behind me as she ran toward the three of us.

Joey loosened his grip but did not let go.

Jessica flew past me and grabbed Joey's arm. "Let go of him! What the hell is wrong with you? Can't you see he can't breathe?" She yanked back on his arm until he released Marcus.

Marcus coughed and grabbed his throat. He slid to the floor next to the elevator, choking and gagging. Jessica knelt next to him. The short white skirt she wore exposed the pink lace thong underneath. Marcus didn't try to hide his stare at her inviting panties.

What a freaking dog. He's on the verge of being choked to death and all he can think of is sex?

"Marc, are you all right?" She grabbed his face, forcing him to look at her.

Marcus nodded but kept coughing and hacking. Jessica checked his neck, rubbing at the red marks from Joey's elbow. She looked up at me. I hadn't moved from my spot. "Why didn't you stop him, Autumn? What's wrong with you?"

Water dripped from Marcus's bulging eyes. Jessica's glare snapped me out of my trance. I knelt next to her. "I think I was in shock. Marcus said…then Joey pushed him…he was turning blue…" I glanced at Marcus. "Are you okay?"

His coughs lessened, but when he tried to speak, the words sounded like gravel. He nodded again.

I pulled my hand back and slapped his cheek, stinging my fingers in the process. My hand painted a red outline on his smooth skin. "Maybe next time you won't be so mean to Joey. He's right. You are a jerk."

I got up and walked over to Joey. His face was red and beaded with sweat as he leaned against a glass wall across from the elevator. His chest heaved with each breath. Watching him fight for me like that and put Marcus in his place set my every nerve ending on fire.

I threw my arms around him and kissed him hard. He hesitated at first, then held me tight against him and returned the hungry kiss. I could feel his heart racing under his shirt. I stretched on my toes to hug him and closed my eyes.

He whispered in my ear through heavy breaths. "It's okay. Everything's all right. We're fine. Don't worry." He rubbed my back as he spoke and kept my body snug against his. "I'll take care of everything."

I took a deep breath and opened my eyes. With night surrounding the ship, I could see the elevator behind us reflected in the glass.

Next to it, I saw Jessica kissing Marcus on the floor. His hand trailed up her overexposed leg.

Ugh. How could she be with him knowing what a jerk he is? "Jessica, take it to the bedroom. Please."

Marcus laughed at me. "Yeah, like we did? On Joey's toolbox at midnight was the farthest from the bedroom we could've gone, don't you think?"

I pushed away from Joey and exploded. "I never touched Marcus!"

Marcus laughed. "Right. Keep denying it so your loser boyfriend believes it. As a matter of fact, are you sure that kid is Joey's and not mine?"

I shook my head and turned to Joey. "He's full of shit, Joey. Emmie belongs to us. I swear, nothing happened with Marcus. I just met him when we boarded the ship!"

Jessica and Marcus both shot me incredulous looks.

I stared at them for a moment, turned on my heel, and grabbed Joey by the hand. I dragged him down the hall and away from Jessica and Marcus as fast as my feet would allow.

My trip into Psychoville just kept getting worse and worse.

I didn't stop dragging him until we made it to my cabin. I opened the door, shoved him in, and locked it behind us. When I turned, I could see tears trickling down his cheeks, reflecting the light from Jessica's open laptop.

"Joey, I don't know what to say. I never slept with Marcus." And I really hadn't. But I had nothing. Nothing I could say would change this. With Marcus saying I had, and Jessica concurring with her silent glare, how could I deny it any longer? He collapsed on the floor in front of me and covered his face in his hands. I jumped to his side. He looked so pathetic, tears sprang to my eyes. Now, we were both crying.

"You're all I ever wanted. I was willing to give you the benefit of the doubt before, but come on, do you think I'm stupid?" He swiped away his tears with the back of his hand. "They both said you were with Marcus. Jessica wouldn't lie even if that douchebag would. And I've seen you stare at him, Autumn. If I can't have you, I don't want anyone. I have no reason to live without you."

I grabbed his arm. "Don't say that! You have a lot to live for! Your family, your job, your friends. I don't deserve a great guy like you, Joey. I never did and I never will. You can hate me for the rest of my life. Just, please, don't say you have no reason to live." Panic welled up inside me. I remembered feeling that way on many occasions. Mom's accident, Dad's accident, Dad's funeral…

But something had always pulled me back. Nisha would bring me a surprise at work, or Jessica would make hot dogs for dinner and put on a chick flick. Sleepy would lick my toes. Or the sun would shine just right into my room, making the perfect ray of light. Those little things made me realize why it was important to keep on living.

Now I knew what Joey needed. He needed the words. Even if I didn't mean them, I had to save him from this pain. For his sake, I had to stop being a selfish bitch.

I took his chin in my hand and turned his face toward mine. "You can have me. I mean, you do have me. I'm yours, Joey. I married you, didn't I? Doesn't that tell you how I feel?" It sounded so weird to have those words tumble out of my mouth. They tasted wrong, but to Joey they would be right.

"What about Marcus?"

I looked away from his forlorn face. I had no idea what was happening with Marcus. Looking Joey in the eye, the lie didn't come as easy as I'd hoped. "Let's forget about him and the past, Joey. Start new. I hung out with him before we got together—"

"You told me nothing ever happened with him. Now you're admitting it did? Forget it." He scrubbed his hand down his face and got up. He walked past me and opened the door.

"Joey, don't leave. Come on, let's talk about this." I reached out toward him, but his long stride carried him away faster than I could grab him. "Maybe we can move away together, start new."

He didn't answer. I followed him out of the room, down the hall, and out the doors toward the back of the ship. The wind was fierce, whipping me with my own hair for what I'd done. Joey marched toward the rail despite the incredible gale force. On a ship this huge, Joey had found the one spot that was isolated. Not a single soul was in sight.

He unbuttoned his shirt and kicked off his shoes.

"Joey, stop! What are you doing?" I bent down and picked up his shoes.

He turned back to me with the most haunting expression I'd ever seen on a living person. No matter how hard I tried, I could not tear my eyes away from his face.

"I can't live like this, Autumn. There's nothing left inside of me." He pointed over his shoulder toward the vast ocean. "That's how I feel inside. Like a great big pool of dark nothing. You're better off without me, anyway. You can do so much better than some dumb grease monkey who barely graduated high school. In fact, you deserve better."

He slipped off his shirt. The wind stole it from him and dragged it out to sea. "I'll love you forever. Don't ever forget that." He stepped up to the rail and grabbed it with both hands.

I ran to catch up to him and clutched his arm. "Joey, please." Tears streamed down my face as I realized his intentions. "Please, don't leave me. I love you. You know that!" I shook his arm. "Please, let's talk this through!"

He released the rail with one hand and wiped the tears from my cheeks. His touch felt like angels' wings gently beating against my skin. I took his hand and held it to my face.

"Don't go. I'm begging you. I know I need you. Stay with me." I grasped at whatever straws I could find. "And Emmie needs you, Joey. You don't want her to grow up without a good dad, do you? Please. Don't do this."

His lips dipped into a frown. "I wish I could believe you. Take care of our baby. Goodbye, Autumn Rayne."

He yanked his hand from my face and climbed onto the rail. I ran up behind him and wrapped both arms around his waist, using every ounce of strength in my sad body to hold onto him.

He pried my fingers off his body, shoved me back, and, before I could get to him, jumped over the edge into the black ocean below.

Thirteen

Joey had jumped over the edge because of what I had done to him. The agony inside of me felt like someone had ripped my heart out, tossed it in a food processor, and shredded it like cheese. The stringy remains weren't enough to sustain my life. There had to be a special corner of Hell reserved for people like me. How many lives would I destroy in the process of ruining my own?

I already messed up Mom and Dad's lives, and Jessica's. I hoped Sir Sleepsalot thought he had a good life. If he didn't, it was because of me, too. This was exactly the reason I kept people away.

I clutched at the railing and screamed Joey's name over and over, searching the blackness below for any movement, any sign that his life remained intact. Panicked, I whirled around to run for help and found Dr. Hardy standing on the top stair of the stairwell, watching me. Her expression resembled a teacher watching a student after an important lesson.

I had no idea what that lesson was.

I ran toward her, begging her to help me, to help Joey, but she remained still, almost statue-like. As I started to plead for her help, I slipped on a wet spot, fell down the stairwell and hit my head. All I could remember after that was being dragged back to my room and crying until I'd expelled every last drop of water that wasn't absolutely necessary to keep me alive. I passed out before Jessica came back—if she even came back at all.

The pillow might still have been damp when I woke up the next morning, or it might just have been my imagination. I had no idea who had put me in my bed or how I had even gotten there. I wasn't even sure of my own name anymore.

Today was my last day in the Bermuda Triangle. I was afraid to get out of bed. What if today was as messed up as every other day had been?

What if—God forbid—it was worse?

I sat up and stared out the window. The dark blue water looked like sparkling sapphires. The light blue sky held cotton ball clouds. The sun shone a brilliant yellow. The island's docks already bustled with cruise ship passengers and locals.

What had happened to Joey? If he was dead because of me, I'd never be able to live with myself. I needed to find out if he was okay.

My pulse reacted to the thought of seeing him again. The obvious thrill on his face when he saw me, the smile he reserved only for me, and the way he tried to act cool but failed were all growing on me.

Jessica stirred on the couch. She opened her eyes and saw me looking at her. "Hey." I pointed out the window, trying to hide my moist eyes. "Beautiful island."

She stretched. "Amazing, isn't it? How do you feel today?" The dark circles under her eyes made me wonder how she felt, not me.

I narrowed my eyes at her. "Not up to talking about it. You?"

She got up and came over to me, then put her hand on my forehead. We weren't the touchy-feely type, so the gesture surprised me. "No fever today. Good job. Let's get your IV drip started early so we can enjoy the sun a little before we go home."

I stared at her face. IV drip? What was she talking about?

This sounded worse than the past two days put together.

The panic from last night shot through my stomach. Nausea gripped my insides. I scooted down under the covers and wrapped my arms around my belly and held it tight, hoping to keep whatever was in it where it belonged.

Jessica grabbed my arm. "What is it? Are you okay?"

I grimaced as the nausea fought to gain control over me.

She tugged on the arm she held. "God, Autumn, talk to me. You're turning green. Is it the nausea again?"

I nodded, afraid to open my mouth for fear of losing last night's dinner.

She pulled a stuffed backpack out of a drawer and dumped a bunch of medical items onto the bed next to me. Needles, bags with yellow liquid in them, alcohol wipes, Band-Aids, and other things I didn't recognize tumbled into the pile. She picked out a tiny container and stabbed the top with a needle.

"Give me your butt, Raynie. This will take care of that nausea. Then we can start your medication, okay?"

Fear replaced the nausea. I held up my hands to stop her.

"Um, Jessica? What is that?" I nodded toward the now-full syringe in her hand. "I don't want to get stuck with any needles. And I don't want to give you my butt." Hoping to keep my butt unstabbed, I pulled my covers closer and tucked them in around my body.

She shook her head. "You have to get the drip today. Please, don't make me force you. You know you need it. You always feel better after the nausea medicine, too, so roll over. Come on." She pulled my covers off my legs, exposing yellow, green, and blue bruises. Some were the size of pencil erasers. Others were as big as oranges.

Shocked, I rolled onto my side. She yanked down my panties and wiped a spot with snow-cold alcohol pads. When she jabbed the needle into my butt, I yelped.

"Sorry, honey. I hate causing you more pain." She gently patted the fire that was now spreading from the needle stick. It didn't help.

I rolled back to face her. "Rephrasing, Jessica. Why do I have to get the drip? What is it for?" I rubbed my butt.

"Because the cancer won't take the day off, so neither should you." She uncapped a needle with her teeth. "And I promised Mom I'd make sure you took all your medicine. I intend to keep that promise."

Holy shit. I had cancer?

Why should I be surprised? I deserved cancer.

I threw my head back against my pillow and noticed a few strands of hair on the sheets. I reached up to my head and pulled my fingers through hair that felt like straw. My hands were covered in hair that had just fallen out.

I stared at my hands and started to cry.

"Aw, honey, please don't cry." Jessica sat down and put her arms around my shoulders. "You're going to be fine, all right? We will fight this thing. What do you say? You and me against the world. You're beautiful no matter what happens to your stupid hair."

I pulled back to look at her. "You can say that because you're sitting there with your pretty blonde hair and great face and know that guys will still want you and you aren't dying. I'm getting bald and bruised and ugly right before my eyes!"

The reality of my predicament held my chest like a vise. My breaths rushed in and out of me as I struggled to keep air in my lungs.

She patted my thigh. "I'm sorry. You're right. Calm down, please. I don't know how you feel, but I know you. And no matter what, we'll always be sisters, and I'll do anything in my power to make you better. Got it?" She smiled at me and rubbed my arm. "Now let me start your IV. We can get the chemo and antibiotics over with and maybe have a little fun if you feel okay. What do you say?"

What could I say? I swiped a tear away with my finger. "Fine. Do what you have to do."

I extended my arm toward Jessica and saw the needle marks. Hey, at least it wasn't from drugs. Or was it? I had no idea. I also had a rash that I didn't recognize. Flipping through my mental filing cabinet of rashes, nothing came up that resembled this.

I pointed to the tiny red bumps on my arm. "Jessica, what's that?"

She lightly rubbed the bumps. "It's from the chemo. It'll go away when treatment is over. Don't worry. It's not permanent."

I was on the verge of giving up trying to figure everything out. One thing I knew for sure—I didn't want this to be my life. I didn't know how I would deal with cancer and dying. With what I'd experienced with my parents, I'd had enough of illness and death to last twenty lifetimes.

But if this trip didn't end soon, I was going to die.

Either from the cancer or from insanity.

"Jessica, what did you say about Mom?"

"I said she only let us come on this trip with her if you promised to take your medicine. And hey, don't forget about the hot-dog eating contest near the main pool today!" Jessica's smile and eyes seemed just a little too wide. "Your favorite!"

I looked down at my arm. "Can I eat hot dogs with this?"

She laughed. "You can eat whatever you want. You might not have much of an appetite, though."

"Jessica, how am I allowed to travel with all this?" I asked, sweeping my hand toward the pile of medical paraphernalia. "I mean, shouldn't I be in the hospital or something?"

She shook her head and forced a tight smile. "Dr. Campbell said you could travel if you took your medicine, avoided sick people, and used your sanitizer religiously. And since this is your second round of chemo and we know how your body reacts and have things under control, he cleared you."

She dropped her gaze and her eyes filled with tears.

"Jessica, can I—"

She shot up and ran into the bathroom. A second later, she blew her nose.

And that probably meant that what she'd said was total bullshit and this would be my last vacation.

Ever.

A soft knock at the door interrupted Jessica. She walked toward the peephole and looked out.

"Who is it?" I asked. Did I even want to know?

She looked over her shoulder and smiled at me. "Ooh! It's Marcus!"

Great. "Don't let him in. I don't want to see him." I'd just woken up, my hair looked like a half-shaved rat's nest, and there were drugs and needles all over the place.

Jessica reached for the door handle. "I'll tell him to go away till we're done. Okay?"

"Tell him I'll meet him at the buffet when my medicine is finished."

She narrowed her eyes at me and walked to my side. "Come on, Autumn. You know I like him. Why would he be meeting you at the buffet?" She covered up the paraphernalia on the bed. "Now get ready for your medicine, and I'll get rid of him."

She cracked the door open just enough to whisper to him. I strained to hear what she was saying. If I was right, it sounded like she was flirting with him.

I had to admit, listening to them made me a little jealous. And annoyed. I had always thought Jessica was prettier than me, but I had better luck with guys. Now she was getting the guys? One of the guys who'd spent the cruise chasing me, not her?

I knew it. I was going to end up alone with my cat. One day, someone would find me dead in my apartment with cats eating me because I hadn't fed them. That was, if anyone bothered to check on me.

And now with me being sick and hairless, it was ending before it began.

She shut the door and came back to the bed. Her eyes sparkled as she dug through the medical stuff and found another needle, which she inserted into my arm after putting on gloves that smelled like burning chemicals. I was amazed that it didn't hurt. Maybe it was because she was good, or maybe it was because my arm had grown used to being violated.

"You're getting so good at this. I'm proud of you. You used to cry every time the IV went in." She hooked it up to a bag of bright yellow liquid. "Maybe I'm just that good though, huh?" She laughed.

I didn't. "How long will this take, Jessica?"

She watched the medication flow through the tubing. "Same as always. I'm going to get ready while it runs." She grabbed a book out of her bag and tossed it to me. I blinked as it came at my face but caught it before it took my eye out. "Here. Flip through this while I'm in the bathroom. You're almost done with it."

The book was titled *Cancer and You: A Young Survivor's Guide*. The creased pages held coffee stains and cat hair. Highlighted text on most pages glowed yellow, and notes in my handwriting filled corners and blank pages. Guess the cancer was an ongoing thing. I flipped through, looking for answers to questions like what kind of cancer did I have? How long would I live? And would my hair grow back?

After spending five minutes reading words that made me sick to my stomach, I slammed the book shut.

What difference did it make anyway? Hopefully the pattern would continue and this would all be over tomorrow, one way or another. Either I'd be stuck with the cancer and learn about it anyway, or things would be different again.

I'd have to wait till tomorrow to find out.

Jessica emerged from the bathroom in a tiny black thong bikini. She was exposing more skin than a stripper. At least my bikini bottom covered my ass.

"Isn't that a bit risqué? One jump in the pool and your boobs will be displayed like in a *Girls Gone Wild* video."

She smiled and pulled on a loose-knit cover-up, then turned to me, spreading her arms out. "Better?"

"That doesn't do much to cover things up, either."

She shrugged. "I like my body. Why not show it off on vacation?" She must have noticed the way I was glaring at her because she huffed. "God, Autumn, what? So I'm proud of all the working out I do. Why can't I be a little wild? This trip is almost over anyway. I want to have a little fun before we dock back in Jersey and reality sets in."

"How long have you liked Marcus?" I asked.

"I met him when we boarded the ship. You introduced us, remember? When I asked if you were interested, you said I could have him." She looked at the medicine bag and walked over to me. She gave the bag a squeeze. "Almost done. Ready for some fun on our last day in Bermuda?"

I nodded. "Am I allowed to have fun with all this?" I pointed toward the medicine and needles.

She kept her eyes on the bag of medication. "Sure. We can do whatever you want." She injected some clear fluid into the IV once the yellow stuff was gone. "And I'm sorry about Marcus. I didn't mean to get mad about that."

"It's fine. I just…" I didn't know what I wanted to say. "How long do I have, Jessica? Am I dying? Like, right now?"

She took a deep breath and sighed. "Don't think like that! You'll go into remission and be just fine." She turned away and busied herself with packing up the drugs. She sniffled and dripped tears onto the backpack as she worked.

Yup, I was definitely dying. Maybe not right then, but it didn't sound too good. I hoped I had at least one more day, because I wanted to get out of the Triangle before it took my life.

I tried to sort through my thoughts, figure out if there was a pattern to the different realities I'd been suffering through, but it was hard to think when my arm felt like I'd just stuck it into a fireplace. "Ouch!" I yelled. "It's burning, Jessica. Fix it."

Jessica shook her head and disappeared into the bathroom again.

Guess it was supposed to burn.

I did a mental tally of my body, pressing on everything from head to toe. Everything seemed to feel okay. Nothing hurt. How sick could I be? I felt around for lumps and looked for scars. Nothing but bruises. I reached up and touched my head. More clumps of hair fell out. I must have looked like those hairless dogs with tiny sprouts of hair here and there.

"Jessica?" I called to her from the bed. My voice broke as I spoke. "Do I have something to cover my head with? A hat or something?" Tears slid down my cheeks as I stared at the loose strands littering the bed.

When I'd heard about Joey taking care of his mother when she had cancer, I couldn't imagine being the patient or the caretaker. Both scared the hell out of me. But being sick scared me the most.

If this day became my reality after the cruise, I couldn't handle it. I wouldn't.

Jessica came out of the bathroom in time for another knock at the door. "Oh God, I hope it's not Joey again. He sure takes the protective brother thing to extremes, especially since he's only a stepbrother." She peeked through the peephole again.

Joey. I'd forgotten all about his plunge overboard last night. Thank God he was alive. But Jessica just said...

I grabbed my hair and shut my eyes. Our stepbrother? Shit. Guess Mom got remarried. Or Dad? Who knew.

I gave up.

He knocked again, harder and louder.

"Autumn's getting her medicine! Come back later!"

"Come on, Jessica. I won't be long. I just want to make sure she's okay," he said through the door.

Jessica glanced at me. "Do you want me to let him in?"

I shrugged. "Just give me a second to—"

I saw his face a second later when she cracked the door open and he pushed past her, his eyes fixed on mine. She retreated into the bathroom again and locked the door behind her.

I pulled the covers over my head. "Get out of here, Joey! I'm not decent!" The last thing I wanted was for any guy to see my ugly head without hair. How could he stand to look at someone so hideous? I didn't even want to see myself.

"You know I don't care about that. How are you feeling?" He sat down on the bed next to me and tugged lightly at the covers, but I held them tight.

"Joey, rephrasing. Get out! I'm hiding here, in case you didn't notice."

"Calm down, Autumn. I'm not going to make you come out of your tent. Tell me you're okay and I'll go. I had to check on you." I heard him open a bag. "And here. This is for you."

I felt the covers move next to my arm. A baseball cap that said "Bermuda" appeared at the end of Joey's hand.

I took the hat, shoved what hair I had up inside it, then lowered the covers. Joey sat next to me. He looked at ease despite the needles and pills spread out on the bed. And despite my damaged head and body.

"Thanks for the hat. I'm hanging in there, I guess." I couldn't look at his eyes. I knew this cancer had to be punishment for every bad thing I'd ever done. "And I'm glad you're okay, too."

Boy, was that an understatement—I thought he might be dead. But he didn't need to know that.

He motioned toward the bathroom with his head. "How's Jessica doing? Is she going out with Marcus today?"

I blinked a few times. "Uh, I think so. Why do you ask?"

His face clouded over. "I just don't like her hanging out with him."

"Why not?"

"Because I don't trust him. He's a player, Autumn. He takes what he can get and moves on. I hate that. Guys like him piss me off."

"How do you know he's a player?"

"He works at the bank by the shop, remember? We've both seen him in the store with different girls. And I bank there, so I've seen how he hunts down women. Every time I go in there he has a different girl hanging around his desk."

Shocker. "Um, how's Emmie today?"

"Who?"

I glanced around the room. No baby stuff. Maybe today Emmie was someone else's baby. "Never mind."

"Almost done," Jessica yelled from the bathroom, her voice an octave higher than usual. "Stop bothering her, Joey. She needs her medicine and her strength."

We both looked toward the bathroom door as it swung open. I wasn't the only one who noticed how great Jessica looked.

"Hey, Jessica. Having fun on vacation?" His eyes popped out of his head as he took in my attractive sister in her itty-bitty bathing suit. I had the sudden urge to beat the crap out of him. And her.

She smiled and nodded. "I have to unhook Autumn, do you mind?" She pulled him off the bed by the arm and dragged him to the door.

He opened the door and paused. "See you guys later." The look he gave us made it clear he'd make sure of it.

Jessica slammed the door and huffed. "He's so annoying. He may as well be our real brother, not just our stepbrother. Did he upset you?"

By the way he had drooled over her, yes, he did. "No. Just get this shit off me, okay? I'm so done."

"Give me your arm." She didn't wait for me to stretch it out toward her. She put gloves back on and yanked it off the bed and got busy pulling out the IV and taping up the needle hole.

I stared out the window as she worked, tears threatening to reveal my true feelings. No one would ever want me like this. Not even Joey. He was probably just pitying me. After all the times I'd called him annoying, he'd been nothing but nice to me on this ship. Every day, every time he saw me. Even when he didn't know me, he was still polite.

When I compared him to Marcus, the contrast was amazing. Marcus only cared about looks and sex.

Jessica cleaned up in silence, then grabbed her beach bag. "I'll see you at the buffet when you're ready. Take it slow, okay?"

I nodded. She waved as she left and closed the door behind her.

I reached up to take the hat off just as the door pushed open. I dropped my hand and looked toward the door, assuming it was Jessica. "Forget something?" I asked.

"Yeah, Snuggle Piggy. I forgot to say I love you." My dad walked in and smiled.

If the nuttiness of the past few days hadn't prepared me to expect the unexpected, I was sure I would've passed out cold. Instead, I sat on the bed with my jaw hanging open and my eyes fixed on him, unblinking and full of tears.

"Daddy?"

He looked just like I remembered, with dark brown, close-cut hair, stunning green eyes, and a masculine jaw. Dressed in Bermuda shorts and a red Hawaiian shirt, his style matched the other passengers on the ship. I thought he was taller, but then again, I'd been much smaller when he'd died.

He sat next to me on the bed and smiled. "How're you doing today, Piggy?"

I'd forgotten that Dad called me Snuggle Piggy. He'd said I was bright pink and stuffed inside my blankets when I came home from the hospital, and I reminded him of a snuggled piglet. Mom never liked it, but I loved it. And hearing it now was like hearing the sound of birds in spring after being deaf all my life.

For this, I would keep the cancer. I would give my life to have my dad back.

He reached out to hug me, but hesitated as his eyes noticed the loose strands of hair on my pillow and a bruise on my arm. I lurched forward and pulled him to me with my bony arms, holding on so tight it hurt, but I didn't care. Tears flowed down my cheeks in rivers. He held me gently, rocking me and rubbing my back.

"Daddy, I can't believe you're here. How did this happen?"

He chuckled in my ear. "Well, I did this amazing thing. It's called making a reservation. And once I paid with a credit card, I got a confirmation number. Then, like magic, I got to take this cruise!"

The door pushed open, and Jessica walked in. "Hey guys. Forgot my camera." She plucked it off the table and slipped her wrist through the strap. She grabbed the door handle and paused, turning to stare at us.

I almost thought she was going to pass out as she focused on Dad, but she narrowed her eyes at him. "Don't bother her for too long. She needs some rest."

"Yes, Mommy Dearest." He shooed her away. "Go have some fun, honey. I'm chatting with Autumn, but I promise to let her get some rest soon. I have a flight home scheduled for later this afternoon."

Bother me for too long? I would stay in this bed and talk to Dad till the cruise police forced me out. At gunpoint. And even then I would put up a pretty damn good fight.

I still hadn't let go of him. "No, Dad, I don't mean how did you make the reservation. I mean…never mind. You cannot imagine how happy I am to see you. If I had to trade my life for this moment, I would."

He unwrapped my arms from around him and gave me a stern look. "Autumn Rayne, don't you ever say that. You hear me? My life is nothing without you in it."

His words made my tears flow faster. "I feel the same way, Daddy. I want to spend every single day I can with you."

"Don't cry, Autumn. I've still got a few sick days I can probably use. Maybe I'll call my doctor and see if he'll write me a note for a few days off, if I tell him my back is hurting again. At least that car accident on your seventh birthday was good for something."

My blood screeched to a halt in my veins. He couldn't mean the accident I caused, could he?

I threw my arms around him again, tears streaming. "I'm sorry," I sobbed into his shirt. "It was completely my fault." A few more tears made their way to my chin. He wiped them off with the edge of my blanket. "I've felt so terrible about that all these years."

He pinched my cheek and frowned. "Why on earth would you think that was your fault?"

"Because you were rushing home to get to my stupid birthday party since I wouldn't start without you. If it wasn't for my birthday, you wouldn't have gotten in that accident. And you and Mom would still be together and happy with me and Jessica."

He hugged me so tight, I thought we were becoming one person. "Autumn, I'm sorry you thought that, but you're wrong. A drunk driver hit me head on. It was never your fault and had nothing to do with your birthday. Who told you that?"

"No one had to. I just knew it. If it wasn't for me, you'd still be here."

He chuckled. "I am here, Piggy. What do you mean?"

How could I tell him he was dead? I couldn't, because I didn't want him to be. "Never mind. I'm just so incredibly happy to see you."

He looked toward the door and said, "Maybe I'd better get Jessica. You don't sound so good." He started to get up off the bed, but I grabbed his arm and held him with all my strength.

"No! Don't go. I'm fine. Hang out with me, please. Stay here forever."

He relaxed and stayed on the bed. "Autumn, I'm just worried sick about you. I love you so much, honey. And maybe this cancer thing wouldn't be happening if it wasn't for me." His eyes welled up with tears.

My shock left me speechless. He felt guilty about me? He had it backwards. "What on earth could you possibly feel guilty about with my cancer, Dad? That kind of thing isn't anyone's fault!"

A tear slid down his cheek. He wiped it away with the back of his hand. "Autumn, you told me you didn't feel good, and I just thought it was the flu, and if I'd taken you to the doctor sooner…" He didn't finish the thought.

I shook my head with as much force as I could. "Don't you dare feel bad, Dad. You let that go right now, you hear me?" Geez, I sounded like Jessica. "I know how it feels to carry around that guilt. All this time I thought your accident was because of me, and I've suffered for it."

He rested his cheek on my head. "No, honey. It was the drunk driver's fault. Not yours. Never yours."

I gulped down a huge breath of scented air. Years of guilt and punishing myself melted away at that moment, making me feel lighter than I had in years. There were no words to describe how it felt to know I hadn't caused his death. I closed my eyes, burning his words into my brain. It wasn't my fault. It wasn't my fault. As the words became more solid, I smiled.

I opened my eyes, confused. "Are we still in Bermuda, or is this Heaven? Or did I go crazy?"

He chuckled. "This is Heaven, Snuggle Piggy. Every father-daughter chat is heaven to me."

I leaned back against my pillow and stared at him. All I wanted to do was drink in everything about him. His face. His cologne. His gestures. If the Bermuda Triangle kept bringing people I loved back to the land of the living, I was jumping ship and staying here forever.

Dad smiled and stood. "Well, I'd better let you rest, and go spend some time with Jessica before I have to go to the airport. She tends to get just a little jealous with all the time I spend with you. Okay?"

"Why are you flying home? You can't stay?"

"No, honey. I had planned on taking the whole cruise, but something came up at work that I have to take care of, so I booked the flight this morning. But we'll hang out again soon, okay?"

I reached for him, but dropped my hand. Not knowing if I'd ever have another chance, I opened my mouth and let my heart spill out. "Daddy, before you go, I just want to tell you that I love you. I always have and I always will, until the day I die and even after that. And I'm sorry for anything I ever did to make you mad or upset with me. And I'll remember this moment for the rest of my life as the most perfect moment ever."

He drew in a shaky breath and plopped onto the bed, wrapping his arms around me before his butt landed on the bedspread. We hugged and cried for what seemed like years.

Which was fine with me. I was making up for lost time.

He released me and stood again, then kissed my cheek. "I'll see you later, okay? You get better. Promise me you will do whatever it takes to get better."

I nodded. "You got it, Daddy. I promise."

He smiled at me, brushed my cheek with his finger, then walked out of the cabin.

I blinked twice, then the floodgates opened. I yelled and screamed, hit my pillow, yanked out some more hair, and screamed again.

What if I didn't get to speak to him ever again and this was my only chance? I cried and cried until it felt like there was no liquid left anywhere inside my body. No one should ever have to suffer the kind of pain I experienced the moment he shut the door on me. My heart hurt so bad, I thought it would leak out of my chest and forget to keep me alive. In fact, I'd hoped it would do just that. I threw my face into my pillow and waited for death to take me.

I got out of bed hours later and was hit with a wave of vertigo. I had to sit and wait out the spinning in my head before I could put on my swimsuit. When I looked in the mirror, I almost hit the floor. My once-thick hair looked like an abandoned bird's nest. My skin was the color of Nisha's Gatorade. Ugly skin sagged off my bones in places I never knew had bones. I ripped off the bathing suit and pulled on a pair of jeans and a T-shirt. I looked like a poorly wrapped Christmas present.

But I didn't care. Because I got to hug my dad one more time. Tell him I loved him one more time. And talk to him, hear his voice…

Nothing compared to that.

I hoped the truth about his death was real, not just this craziness I'd been living through. If I truly wasn't responsible…I'd have to ask Jessica about it. It would change my life.

I grabbed my beach bag and threw some books into it. Whatever Jessica had put in me took my appetite away, but I still went to the buffet to grab a little something and search for her and the guys. I couldn't believe how slow my steps were. I couldn't believe how sick I felt.

I couldn't imagine living like this every day.

I was down the hallway from the buffet when I heard Jessica's voice. She and Joey chatted outside the restaurant's entrance. I stumbled toward them, still reeling from my encounter with Dad. Jessica saw me first and gasped.

"Autumn, your arm is bleeding where I put in your IV! We need to go back to the room!" Jessica demanded.

I saw the blood and stumbled back. I put pressure on the spot that was bleeding, but the warm, thick liquid made me queasy. "Jessica, help me." I slid down the wall and landed on the cold floor.

Joey was quickly turning green, but Jessica ran over and helped me up.

"Autumn, what are you doing, huh?" She led me back to the cabin and wrapped my arm with some white gauze from the medical supplies. "You've gotta think." She refused to look at me as she worked. "You need to rest as much as you can, especially when you don't feel well. You know that."

"Ow, Jessica, that's tight."

"Sorry. I just don't understand you." She unwound the gauze and wrapped it looser. She finally looked at me. "What's gotten into you? If you don't take better care of yourself, the chemo isn't going to work and you're going to die sooner. Is that what you want?"

I glared at her. "I'm not dead yet. Don't tell me what I can and can't do. I want to live while I still have the chance." Maybe she didn't know me at all, but I was not about to lie down and roll belly-up to this disease. "Besides, you told me to come find you when I was ready, and I was ready."

She softened. "Sorry, I did say that, didn't I?" She taped the gauze in place and looked at me. "Fine. Did Joey want something before?"

I shrugged my thin shoulder. "Not really. But he tried to be sweet while you were in the bathroom by giving me a hat to cover my hideous head. He's kinda decent, don't you think?"

Her eyebrows shot up. "No. Are you forgetting all the times he made Mom cry because he tried so hard to split her and Skip up before they got married? He's gotten better over the last few years, but still. He caused so much heartache in our house. I'm shocked to hear you defend him. Unless..." She stopped talking and put tape on the end of the gauze roll.

"Unless what? Spit it out Jessica, I'm dying, right? Just say it." I pointed to my latest bandage. "I don't have much time."

She put her hand on her right hip and stared at me. "I was going to say, unless you like him?"

Fourteen

I felt the instant rush of heat to my cheeks. "No! I just know Joey's a nice guy, and you know it, too. And you know Marcus is a man-whore. You should totally stay away from him."

Jessica shrugged. "And since when do you care what I do? You never did before."

I sighed. "Since now. I don't want to see you get hurt. Just finish me up so I can get some sun before the damn cruise is over."

She looked at me strangely for a minute, then shrugged. "Fine. You're done." She got up and threw out the medical trash.

I pursed my lips. "And what if I do like Joey?" tumbled out of my mouth before I could stop it. I think I looked as shocked as she did when I said it.

"Mom will be pissed." Jessica smiled at the thought. "She thinks he's too much trouble after everything he put her through. Mom knows he's interested in you, and she isn't happy about that."

"Why was he such a jerk to her?" I asked.

She washed her hands and ignored my question. "I'm going to get ready for the pool. You coming?"

"Rephrasing here. What did Joey do?" I asked. "Answer me."

She pursed her lips. "Come on, we'll talk later. Who wants to go over that crap yet again? Let's get to the pool. You feel okay to go? We can relax in those big chaise lounge chairs."

I nodded and followed her out the door. Why wouldn't she tell me what Joey did? Was it that bad?

At the pool, while walking among the crowds, I scanned the area for Joey and Marcus. No sign of either of them. That was a good thing.

"Here's two together. Is this okay?" Jessica asked, gesturing toward two chairs near the elevators.

I shrugged. She sat on one chair and held my bag for me so I could sit and get comfortable. "We have to take some pictures for Mom. Don't let me forget. And try to look happy, okay?"

I forgot about Mom and this reality's remarriage. "And what's Mom doing now? Is she off with Skip somewhere?" If she was on the ship and I could talk to her too, my life would be complete. I would move into the Bermuda Triangle and spend the rest of my life pretending my parents were okay. Even if I wasn't. Even if I had to have cancer and chemo and falling-out hair every day.

I would put up with all of it to keep them in my life.

"Oh, Autumn, don't start. Everyone knows you hate Skip, but she loves him and he's good to her. They went sightseeing on the island, then extended their trip by staying at a hotel for a few days. They fly home from there. We have to remember to pick them up from Newark, so don't let me forget."

Geez, I just wanted to know if I could talk to her like I'd talked to Dad. "Mom and Dad took the same cruise while Mom is remarried?"

She shot me a glare. "They're grown-ups, Autumn. They tolerate each other. It's not a problem. Why are you acting so shocked?"

I sighed. "Forget it. My brain is just fried. Don't listen to me." I didn't want to get into an argument over what Dad was or was not doing. I wanted to keep that memory of him precious, so I dropped it.

"Hey there. Can we talk?"

I opened my eyes to see Marcus, two drinks in his hands. I started to move to let him sit next to me. But he looked at me the way I looked at Sleepy when I wanted to sit in my favorite chair and he was already there. Except, I wasn't a cat, and Marcus had no right to displace me.

"Oh, sorry, Rayne." He didn't give me a second glance. "Jessica? Can we talk, please?"

Marcus had always drooled over me. He'd noticed me when I didn't even know him. Now he was treating me like I was a part of the chair? Asking for Jessica?

When did I become invisible to him?

Jessica slid her legs up on the chair and motioned for him to sit. I lowered my sunglasses so I could stare without them seeing me.

She tilted her head and smiled at him. "Is that drink for me?"

"Of course." He handed her a sweaty glass with an umbrella floating in it. "Anything for you, beauty."

"Thanks." She took a dainty sip of the pink liquid. "Now, are we hanging out today or are you spending the day with the redhead in the purple thong?"

"She's no one. I met her for dinner, but I didn't tell you because I didn't want to upset you. Because nothing happened, Jessica." He took her hands in his. "She's known my family for years. I told her I wasn't interested in going out, but my mom pushed it." He flashed a dimpled grin that I was sure had melted many hearts before.

I narrowed my eyes at him. Jessica's face appeared calm and unconcerned. She needed a giant smack in the head. If he could so easily sway her, she wasn't as smart as I thought she was.

She pulled her hands away. "I'll have to talk to Joey. He doesn't lie to me." She blinked once. "And you do."

He started to protest, but she put her hand up to stop him. "Hey, Marcus, it's fine. This is vacation. I know how it goes. What happens on the ship, stays on the ship, right? So, whatever. I really don't care what you do. Just don't think you can lie to me and get away with it. Besides, I'm just here to have fun." "You go, girl!" I said. Ha!

He dropped his shoulders and sighed. "Jessica, don't listen to him. He hates me and wants you, so he'll say anything to change your mind. You should realize that."

I sat up. Did he just say Joey wanted Jessica? And if he had, why was I surprised? Maybe they were never interested in me to begin with. Maybe this was all an elaborate scheme to get to my sister.

Note to self—I hate men.

She shrugged. "Whatever."

I slid my sunglasses onto my head. "Jessica, I'm going to walk around a bit. I'll meet you back here. Watch my stuff, okay?"

"Sure," she said. "Don't overdo it, though. Take it easy."

I rolled my eyes at her warning and left.

The comments she'd made earlier about Mom hating Joey had me curious. I searched through the buffet and the pool area before I finally found him sitting alone at the back of the ship, staring off into space. His white tank top made his dark tan stand out. He'd kicked off his flip-flops and crossed his long legs in front of him.

I touched his shoulder. "Hi," I said, somewhat out of breath. Damn, cancer sucked.

He didn't turn around. "Hey."

"What's up with you and Marcus?" I walked around to face him, but his eyes didn't meet mine.

"Forget it. It doesn't matter. He's a jerk."

I knelt in front of him. "It does matter. I don't want Jessica to get hurt. She says she's just out to have fun, but I know her. Her heart is fragile."

He looked out over the vast blue expanse that supported the ship. "I didn't plan on telling you this, but I was walking around late last night, checking out the ship and some of the quieter, deserted areas. I heard some noise coming from behind one of the life boats."

My heart picked up the pace. I knew what he was going to say. Even though this whole time in the Triangle was some twisted fantasy, I still felt inside of me the way a girl feels when a guy cheats on her. Used. Ugly. Worthless. It had happened to me freshman year and ruined my self-esteem for months.

I wanted to run back to the pool deck and beat the crap out of Marcus.

"Marcus was screwing some girl in a corner under the stairs. I thought he saw me, but I just turned away and kept going. I mean, I wasn't going to hang around and watch the show, you know? I can't believe Jessica could want anything to do with a guy like that."

The past three days had worn me down to my last nerve. I'd once heard Mom say she needed a vacation to recover from her vacation. Now I knew what she'd meant.

"Joey, I don't feel so good." I plopped down onto the ground.

He jumped to my side. "What can I do? I'm sorry. I didn't mean to upset you."

"I'm fine. Just do me a favor and help me get to the doctor's office. There's a lady there I want to talk to."

Joey helped me up and walked with me to the infirmary. The girl at the desk had her back to us as she faxed something. A bag of yellow liquid sat on the desk next to her.

My body started to go down. Joey wrapped his arm around my waist and supported me.

"You okay?" he whispered. Concern colored his eyes.

"Can I help you?" the girl asked before I could answer.

"Can I see Dr. Hardy, please?" I asked, my voice a little breathless.

"Who?" She turned, looked at my face and hair, and winced.

I reached up to touch my head. I wanted to make sure my head was still covered with the hat Joey had given me.

"Dr. Hardy. The lady doctor? I saw her the other day. I need to speak to her."

She cocked her head to the side. "Oh, I know who you mean. Sorry about that. Have a seat, please. I'll see if she's available."

I sat while she called someone, glancing at me during the conversation. "Miss? We have two doctors here today, and both are men. Dr. Margaretta and Dr. Turk. Do you want to see one of them?"

I stared at her for a second, then walked away without a word. I willed the cancer to take me now or cut the crap and let me get on with my life.

"Miss Taylor? I can see you now," Dr. Hardy said from behind me. The receptionist raised her eyebrows and shrugged when she noticed Dr. Hardy, then mumbled something about doctors and their schedules.

I turned and followed the pretty doctor into the same exam room I had been in the last time.

She shut the door and took in my appearance. A gasp escaped her pink lips. "What happened?"

I had no time for bullshit. I mustered up my strength and gave her my best glare. "I think you know what happened. Why don't you tell me, before I drop dead of whatever is happening to me."

She put her clipboard down and sighed. She stared at me for a full minute before speaking. "Every cruise, someone walks in here and tells me they think they're going nuts. They worry that the Triangle is to blame. The experiences are different for each person, but I can tell you that you aren't the only one." She leaned closer to me. Her stethoscope smacked me in the shoulder. "Don't tell anyone, but it's happened to me, too."

My eyes widened. "Really?"

She winked and nodded. "I don't tell this to anyone except for my patients like you. If I admitted it to anyone else, they might think I'm crazy.

But people like us—" she pointed to us both "—we know the truth. And sometimes, we get stuck here."

At this point, I didn't care if she told me unicorns and fairies were real. I just wanted answers.

And it looked like she had them.

"So what's going on? Tell me everything." She took a seat across from me and put her hand on my knee.

I had already told her about my parents, Jessica, Joey, and Marcus. Now I added the cancer part, and recapped the rest.

A serious expression crossed her face when I was done. "Listen to me. Things happen in the Triangle that no one can explain. I've been trying to explain what happened to me for years. But don't take these changes lightly. Any day on this ship could become your permanent reality. I can't tell you how it works, but you have to believe me. Do you understand?" The intensity of her green eyes scared me. Her tone took on such a serious edge, I almost burst into tears. "Remember my words. Any changes that happen on this ship can become your life back home. Keep that in mind."

What the hell? I could get stuck in this screwiness forever? And what if I got back to Jersey and everything was different for the worse, not the better? What if…what if? There were so many what ifs, I didn't know where to begin.

I frowned at her. "How come I'm the only one noticing it? Why don't the others realize things are different? And what did I do to deserve this?" Yet I knew what I did. I didn't have to ask.

I ruined lives all around me.

"Whoa, dear, one thing at a time. The Triangle affects everyone differently. Some people change with the changes, some notice weird things, like you did, and some experience nothing out of the ordinary. I'm sorry, honey. I wish I had better news or a simple answer, but I don't." She held out a hand and helped me off the exam table. "Go. Have fun with the rest of your cruise. But think about your life and where you're headed. Think about where you've been. And if you solve the mystery of the Triangle, please drop me a line and let me know, okay?"

I nodded. "Thank you for understanding. I thought you'd send me to a mental hospital or something."

She shook her head. "Never." I reached for the door, but she grabbed my hand with surprising intensity. "Keep searching. I need answers just as much as you do."

"I will," I promised.

Joey caught up to me as I slipped out of the room. "Autumn, what happened?"

I spun to face him. Dizziness gripped me, so I reached out to steady myself against the wall. "Nothing. I'm going to lie down." He grabbed my arm, but I shrugged him off and stumbled down the hall. When I got to the room, I realized my key was in my bag by the pool. I banged my head against the cabin door, hoping to shake loose whatever curse had taken hold of me.

"Autumn, slow down," he called after me. "What's the problem?"

I sat down against the door. I could feel the rocking motion of the ship attempting to comfort me. I put my head between my knees and started crying.

Joey put his arms around my bony shoulders.

"I'm so confused. I'm sick, I'm ugly, I'm…I'm a bad person," I mumbled into my knees. "I just want to make things right."

"Autumn, you're beautiful. Don't talk like that. Once the chemo is over, your hair will grow back. The bruises will go away. Being sick is only temporary."

"And sometimes it's permanent. Who would want me like this?" I pulled some loose strands of hair from my head. I wiggled my fingers and they floated to the floor. "I'm being punished, Joey." I looked at his concerned face. "I…you—"

My words were stifled by his mouth on mine. The desperation in his kiss crushed my desire to push him away, and against my will, I kissed him back. The past few days with him being so sweet to me, and then holding me close on the ship, melted my resolve to deny him. He wrapped his arms around my waist with a gentleness that made me shudder. I grabbed the back of his head and pulled him closer to me. For a moment, I forgot where I was, who I was, and how much was wrong with my life. It was just me and Joey, our kiss, and nothing else.

He broke the kiss before me, but I pulled him to me and planted my mouth on his for another round.

He pulled away and looked at me, his eyes full of wonder and surprise.

"Autumn, you actually kissed me back. I had no idea how you felt." He pressed his lips together for a moment. "I mean, I've been interested in you for a long time, but with your mom and my dad, the things I've done..." He trailed off looking at the floor. "I thought you hated me for making your mom so miserable."

Oh, damn. He had to bring up my mother? For a little while, I'd forgotten about my crappy life back home.

Another wave of guilt slapped me hard across the face. Mom was miserable and sick, and I was making out with Joey. I had to put a stop to this.

He leaned in to kiss me again, but I put my hand on his warm chest to stop him.

"Um, Joey, I'm sorry." I covered my face in my hands. "I didn't mean for that kiss to happen."

He let go of me and got up. I peeked up at him. He opened his mouth to say something as he reached for me, but I tilted away from his arms, and he walked away with his head down.

I sat there for a minute and tried to focus. Did it matter that I had upset him in this weird dimension? Not really. Did it matter that I had kissed him?

Absolutely. More than I realized.

I slowly made my way to the pool deck, stumbling along and breathing hard. When I got there, Marcus was asleep in my chair. Jessica slept beside him with her face covered. I slid my bag out from between the chairs as quietly as possible and tucked myself away in my room. The best option for me at this point was avoidance of everyone and everything. I didn't want to cause any more damage to anyone.

The only person I wanted to see now was my dad. Another chance to talk to him would warm my sad heart. I headed back to the room, knowing he'd check on me again.

If he was still around.

After a long nap, I woke up to darkness. I had no idea how long I'd slept, but Jessica had come in and covered me with a blanket. A tray of cheeses, strawberries, bananas, and grapes sat beside me on the nightstand, along with a bottle of water. More of my hair littered my pillow.

I sat up and turned on the light. After brushing the loose hairs away, I took the books out of the bag and munched on the snacks while I flipped through another one of the Bermuda Triangle books.

A chapter on people who got lost in the Triangle had photographs and captions describing when they had gone missing. It was strange reading about people who had disappeared off the face of the planet. I wondered what really happened to them.

One of the women in a black and white photograph looked familiar. She held an old-fashioned suitcase while boarding a small ship behind her. Her expression was almost terrified, with wide eyes, a half-opened mouth, and pale skin. I wondered what could have scared her so much when it looked like she was just going on vacation. I scanned the caption.

"Twenty-three-year-old Harriett Hardy boards the yacht owned by her fiancé, Richard Templeton, in 1938. The ship disappeared when it entered the Bermuda Triangle on July 26. The ship and occupants have never been located. Miss Hardy was an outspoken believer in the Bermuda Triangle and feared going through it."

I looked closer at the picture. The woman was the same doctor I had seen on the ship. The one I kept running into, with the red hair and green eyes.

Dr. Harriett Hardy.

Fifteen

I slammed the book shut and closed my eyes. Sleep and dreams would never be as bad as the past three days had been. I willed myself to sleep to escape my horrible life.

I was awakened by the door opening, some time later. The book with Harriett's picture still sat next to me on the bed. I focused on the door, wondering what tragedy was walking in now.

Jessica frowned at me. "You okay?" She came over and sat on the edge of the bed. "You never came back." She put her hand on my head to check my temperature.

I sighed. "Joey said Marcus had sex with some girl under the stairs. You don't need a guy like that, Jessica. What are you doing with him?"

She took my hand. "I know, Autumn. Why am I bothering with Marcus?" she asked, more to herself than to me. "Must be some kind of vacation psychosis." She chuckled.

Vacation psychosis? Did that exist? Maybe that was my problem. "What's vacation psychosis?"

She laughed. "A joke, honey. Kidding."

Oh, well. "You never told me what Joey did to Mom. Why does she hate him?"

Jessica sat on the edge of the bed. "Don't you remember? You were there." She shook her head. "He was very upset that his dad started dating Mom so soon after his own mom had, you know. He thought his dad was betraying her memory or something." She leaned over and straightened up the brochure collection on the table. "He tried so hard to break them up that Skip stopping seeing Mom. And Mom was devastated." She got up and started digging through her clothes. "Anyway, it all ended fine because they got back together and Joey calmed down, but she's never been able to let that go. We were all miserable for a while because of him." She shrugged. "But it's in the past. We can't change it, right?" She sighed. "I'm going to the comedy show for a little fun after all this seriousness. Want to come?"

I shook my head. "I'm just going to hang around, maybe get something to eat. Have fun at the show."

Jessica left for the comedy show, and I got dressed. I understood why Joey had done what he did when he was younger, in this reality. The thought of any other man besides my dad, especially after he'd just died, with Mom made me cringe. Dad loved her with all his heart. Picking someone new was the equivalent of going to the pet store and picking out a new puppy the day the last one died.

I couldn't say I blamed him for his attempt at breaking them up. I might have—would have—done the same thing when it was new.

But now, I only wanted to see Mom happy. If a new guy treated her right and loved her, I'd be fine with that. And it looked like Joey had gotten over his selfishness, too.

Thank God.

My stomach grumbled. When was the last time I'd eaten? Taking my dinner to go from the buffet line seemed like a great idea. Eating out by the pool, alone, seemed even better. After I got a roll and chicken noodle soup, I headed outside and made my way to a table near the railing, so I could listen to the sounds of the ocean as the ship sped toward home.

And away from the Bermuda Triangle and this mess I'd been living.

Quiet voices near the pool disturbed the silence. I looked over to see Joey and Marcus arguing. Both of them stood stiffly, arms ready to throw some punches.

I left my food and walked over to them. When they saw me, they stopped talking.

"Guys. What's going on?" I crossed my arms over my chest and looked back and forth between the two of them.

"Nothing, Autumn. Go get some rest," Joey said. "We were just, um, talking."

They glared at each other. "Are we done?" Marcus glared at Joey.

"No. Later." Joey stepped toward me. "Come on, Autumn." He grabbed my hand to lead me away.

Jessica walked around the corner and saw the three of us.

"What's going on, guys? I'm all dressed up with no place to go. Anyone up for the comedy show?"

They both stared at her. I got it that she was beautiful, but the minute she showed up I no longer existed. After both of them had been chasing me before, the way they ignored me now shot down my ego with a bazooka.

Joey dropped my hand. "I was just helping Autumn to the cabin. She needs some rest."

"Why don't you help her with that, and I'll take Jessica to the club," Marcus said. He slipped his arm around her waist and turned her toward the elevators.

Joey tugged on my shirt lightly. "Come on back to the cabin, Autumn."

I turned to him. The pure and innocent look on his face hit me in the gut. Joey didn't deserve the way I'd been treating him since January. He really was different than I'd thought. He was nice. He was sweet. He was one of the last honest guys on the planet.

I was staggered at the realization that Joey meant something to me. And now, with this cancer, I had no time left to act on it.

I lost my grip on the railing and almost fell. He caught me by the arms and steadied me.

"What's the matter?"

I grabbed the railing again. "I really don't care about resting, Joey." A tear slid down my cheek. "I'm as good as gone. If we don't get home soon, I'll die." I looked back at the ocean and the darkness beyond it. "I'm sure of it."

He took my face in his hands. "Autumn, you know how much I care about you. Please don't talk like that. Even if you don't care about me, too, I want you to get better." He dropped his hands from my face and slid them down my neck to my shoulders. "For you, for your mom. For Jessica."

I tried to escape his grip. I didn't want to hear any more, but he held me tight. "Joey, I don't know why you care about me so much after the way I've treated you."

"Autumn Rayne, please. If you think there's a chance for us, even the tiniest chance, tell me. I don't care that you're sick. I just need to know if we can be together."

More tears spilled over my cheeks. I didn't know if my heart could take Joey on. After spending so much time pushing everyone away, I didn't know how to let someone in.

Jessica ran over to me and grabbed my hand, pulling me away from him. "I walk away for ten seconds and turn to see her in tears." Marcus followed behind her, asking her when they were going to the club. Ignoring him, she continued talking to me. "What's going on? Why are you crying?" She glared at Joey as she wrapped her arm around my shoulder. "What did you do to her?"

Joey and I stared at each other. Jessica reached out and shook my arm. "God, Autumn, answer me! What's wrong?"

I released Joey's gaze and looked at Jessica. "I don't want to continue the medication. My life is over anyway, so why bother?" Maybe taking a tumble over the ship like Joey had would end my worries. "Just let me live my last days without all the tubes and IV bags." As I spoke the words, I realized what I was now living—Mom's life. IVs. Liquid life. Bed rest. The final stop? A coffin, just like Dad, if I didn't escape the Triangle before it was too late.

She narrowed her eyes at Joey. "What the hell did you say to her?" She put her hands on her hips. "Giving our parents grief wasn't enough for you? You have to torture my sister, too? Forget the club, Marcus. I'm taking Autumn back to the room."

Marcus stood next to Jessica and glared at Joey. Joey planted his feet, readying for the fight that appeared sure to happen.

Marcus opened his mouth, but Joey cut him off. "Stay out of this, Marcus. You aren't part of this family."

Jessica pulled me behind her toward the elevators. "Let them work it out. I don't want you to get hurt if things get bad. I'll come back and check on them."

I stared at them as she dragged me away and around the corner, stumbling as I fought with myself over whether I should go with Jessica or see what was happening between the guys.

"Wait, Jessica." I stepped up to the corner and peeked around. "I just want to hear what's going on."

"Forget them, honey. You need some rest. Come with me."

As we turned to go, I heard them arguing and stopped. Marcus's voice floated toward me.

"...isn't she your sister? You know, that's kind of sick." He pushed Joey. "Incest is disgusting. What's the matter? Can't find a girl who isn't related to you? Rayne deserves someone better. Someone with money and a way to take care of her." He looked Joey up and down. "That, my friend, is not you."

Joey pushed Marcus up against the rail. They struggled as they both fought to get control of the other. In a tangle of bulging muscles and heavy breathing, they scuffled dangerously close to the edge.

As I watched, I noticed the railing they were fighting against had a gate that was starting to give way. I screamed from where I stood. "The gate's opening! Look out!"

With my stupid illness slowing me down, I got to them just in time to see the gate swing open. Joey and Marcus tumbled over the edge, a jumble of arms and legs struggling against gravity. I heard screams as they fell, voices that were swallowed up in the dark night.

I looked over the edge. Jessica ran up behind me, put her arms around my shoulders, and gasped.

Joey and Marcus lay motionless in a heap on the deck below.

Sixteen

"Oh God, oh God, no!" Jessica screamed. Her words were sucked up by the wind.

I grabbed her arm. "We have to do something, Jessica! We have to help them! Let's go!"

She yanked me away from the edge and ran to the pool area and found the stairs, dragging me behind her.

"Help! My friends just fell over a rail! They're hurt!" I screamed, but no one was around to hear my cries. Where the hell was everyone?

We bounded down the stairs to the site of the fall. It felt like hours, but we must have only been away from the ledge above for a minute or two.

Joey and Marcus remained motionless. I couldn't bring myself to walk over to them to check if they were alive. Death was not something I was good at handling. Especially with the reminder of Dad.

Joey lay on the deck on his back with Marcus slumped across his stomach. Joey's right arm rested next to him, but his left arm was hidden under Marcus's body. Joey's legs jutted out straight from under Marcus.

Blood pooled under Joey's head.

A lot of blood.

Marcus's body seemed to have had the better deal, having landed on top of Joey. But his face had obviously kissed the deck. His hair flopped over his cheek, so I couldn't see how much damage he'd taken, but his head twisted at an odd angle from his neck.

I froze about ten feet from them. Jessica ran to them, kneeling next to the heap of arms and legs that were spread out and bleeding.

She placed a finger on each of their necks and blew out a breath. "It's okay, Autumn. They're both breathing. Come here. Help me."

Though my legs felt like they were made of cement, I made my way toward the bodies. Blood and broken bones didn't rank high on my list of things to experience up close and personally, either.

"I can't see where Joey's cut, and Marcus's neck is not at a good angle. We have to be careful moving him." She glanced around the deck and located an emergency phone. She ran to it and yanked up the receiver, but put it back down a second later. "Freaking great. No dial tone. Stay with them while I go get help. I'll be right back"

I stared down at her without speaking. She wanted me to babysit broken bodies? "Can't you use your cell phone?"

She grabbed my arm and shook it. "Listen to me, Autumn! They need help, and I'm going to get it. Stay here. They need us to be strong, okay? Can you do that? I'll get help quicker just running inside than trying to figure what number to call."

I nodded. I opened my mouth to speak, but nothing came out. My brain was done.

She pulled me down by my arm. "If they come to, make sure they don't move. Tell them help is coming. I'll be back in a minute, okay?"

"Uh, okay," I whispered. She left me kneeling next to them, feeling the most helpless I'd ever felt.

I wanted to cry and scream and run and freak the hell out. But I knew it wouldn't do any good.

So, I sat there and stared up at the stars instead of looking at them. Pretending I was just stargazing on a beautiful ship in the middle of the ocean was easier than facing the lives that hung in the balance at my feet.

Joey groaned. I snapped my head down and opened my eyes wide. Thrusting my hands out in front of me, I lightly grabbed his arm.

"Joey, don't move. You're hurt. Stay still, okay? Jessica's getting help."

He groaned again, and his eyelids fluttered. He reached around to the back of his head and pulled his hand back out.

Blood dripped from his fingers.

As soon as he saw the crimson liquid, he gasped and wiggled under Marcus.

"Joey! Stop moving! You and Marcus are hurt! Lay still." I put my hands on his chest and pressed lightly, hoping to keep him down and calm.

But then Marcus moaned, and Joey noticed Marcus was on top of him. "Get the hell off me!" He growled, now struggling to push Marcus off.

I shoved his chest back down. "Joey, stop! His neck is hurt!"

But Joey didn't hear me, because with one giant shove, he flopped Marcus off him and sat up, pushing my hands away at the same time. His face displayed confusion. "What happened? Where's Jessica? Why am I bleeding?" He glanced around and saw Marcus slumped over next to him. "What's wrong with him?"

I grabbed his shoulders and forced him back down on his back. "Joey, you're bleeding. Stop moving around, dammit! Jessica went to get help." I looked at Marcus, lying still like he'd face-planted after a night of heavy drinking.

"Let me check on Marcus. Lay still."

I got up just as Jessica ran over with two men in white coats.

"Autumn! I told you not to let them move. What happened?"

I watched as the men ran over to Marcus and knelt next to him. One had a black bag with medical equipment in it and the other carried a plastic neck collar like the ones I'd seen in the movies.

A tear escaped my eye. "I tried, Jessica. I told Joey to stop moving but he pushed Marcus off him and he hasn't moved since."

One of the men held Marcus's neck still while the other leaned down and spoke to him. "Sir, can you hear me? Sir? Are you all right?"

Marcus groaned and coughed. When he spoke, it sounded like he was talking into a pillow—probably because his face and the ground shared the same space.

"Sir? Can you talk?"

Marcus coughed once more, slowly turned his head, then opened his eyes. "I can't feel anything below my neck." His words came out dazed and questioning.

Jessica sucked in a breath. "Oh, my God. His neck is broken. Marcus, do not move."

Could Marcus truly be paralyzed? By now, the other man was checking out Joey's head, but Joey could move everything and seemed to be okay. The guy kept Joey on the ground as he examined his head, pointing out the cut on his scalp that bled so much. I watched Joey touch the back of his head, then check out his bloody fingers again.

I burst into tears. If Marcus was paralyzed, it was my fault. Because I hadn't been able to stop Joey from moving him.

I was worthless.

Jessica grabbed me and pulled me from the deck. "Come on. They're being taken care of now. Let's take care of you. We can check on them later, right?" she asked, glancing at one of the men.

He nodded. "The help desk will direct you to the ship's hospital. We'll take them there first and stabilize them. If anything else needs to be done, we'll arrange emergency transport. Are they traveling with you ladies?"

"No, they both came with family. I'll give you their cabin numbers so you can contact each of their families." Jessica passed along all the necessary information while I just tried not to pass out.

Still holding me to her, Jessica dragged me away when she was finished talking to the medical guys. My energy drained like a dying battery. I slowed down and leaned against the wall near the elevators. My breathing was labored.

She grabbed my arm. "What is it?"

I struggled to catch my breath. "I'm losing the battle, Jessica. I'm losing. Tonight has been too much on me."

She slipped her arm around me to keep me steady. "I'm taking you back to the room right now. Don't worry."

"Well, how do we know if they're okay? I'm not sure I want to leave them."

"You heard the medic. They won't do anything without contacting their families first. Plus, you need some rest. Let's take care of you now, huh?" We got on the elevator. I pressed the button for the ninth deck and leaned against the back wall of the elevator, staring at Jessica's back.

I grabbed my head. If this was what insanity tasted like, I preferred real life. Even with all of its faults.

It would be a long time before I took another cruise after this.

Once inside our cabin, Jessica settled me on the bed and gave me a pill she claimed would calm me down.

It didn't. For some reason, it made my mind race, my skin crawl, and my head hurt.

I climbed out of bed and headed toward the door.

"What are you doing? Get back in bed. I have to go find the boys' families in case the ship's staff can't contact them, and I don't have time to chase after you."

I backed away from her, opened the door, and stomped toward the elevators with as much energy as I could muster. My heart pounded in my ears. Cramps riddled my legs. I ran until I made it to the back of the ship, out of view of other people and away from the disaster that my life had become.

Jessica didn't follow. She must've known I needed the space.

At least both guys were alive. Two less people I had to consider casualties of Autumn.

But would Marcus be paralyzed forever? And how much blood had Joey really lost? It looked like a lot to me. Plus, besides what we did know, we had no idea what else they had hurt during their fight and fall.

And they were fighting about me. Again.

This was why I didn't want a boyfriend. It hurt too much to let anyone get close to me, only to see things end like this. Everyone I loved seemed doomed because of the poison that flowed through my veins. Dad was dead because of me. Mom was in a coma because of me. Joey's heart was broken because of me. And Jessica was stuck dealing with a selfish, bitchy teenager.

Me.

All I wanted was to fix things. I really did. I just didn't know how. The only thing I could think of that would make everything better for everyone else would be taking myself out of their lives.

I climbed onto the ledge and steadied myself. I peered down at the vast ocean. It beckoned me to join it.

What could it hurt to jump? Maybe it would be like bungee jumping or jumping out of an airplane. Maybe it would feel like riding a roller coaster. Maybe it wouldn't hurt as much as my life did. And since none of this trip was real, maybe it would just knock some sense into me and I could wake up to what I knew—my life.

A thought occurred to me. As I suffered through each day and had no control over what was happening, nothing I'd done or said changed things. What if jumping was the answer to resetting my life?

To make everything right again?

"Autumn, don't!" I thought I heard Joey scream as I took a deep breath, spread my arms wide, and leaned into the darkness.

The wind bit my face. I kept hearing Joey's voice call my name over and over, his voice losing volume as the distance between us increased. The weightless feeling as I floated through the air, the desire of gravity to take me, and the feeling of freedom from my life settled a calmness over me I hadn't felt in years.

My final thought was to wonder how Joey was calling for me when he was in the hospital. Maybe it was a hallucination, and I just wanted him to want me.

To need me.

To love me.

Finally, icy pain and darkness ended everything that was Autumn Rayne Taylor.

Seventeen

"Get up, you bum." Jessica's voice, muffled as if it were spoken through cotton, sounded irritated.

I slowly opened my eyes and blinked a few times. Sunlight streamed in through the cruise ship window, showering my face with heat. I glanced over at Jessica. She was brushing her hair into a sassy ponytail. The pink sundress she wore added to the innocent little girl picture she was painting.

I coughed, and the taste of salt water stung my tongue. The events of the night before hit my brain like a deadly virus. I shot up in bed and gasped.

Jessica dropped the brush and looked at me. "What's wrong?"

"What day is it?" I asked.

"Thursday. It's the last day of the cruise. We left Bermuda last night and will spend today at sea." She picked up the brush and fluffed her ponytail. "Why?"

I shook my head, attempting to clear out the memory of my leap over the edge of the ship. I could feel and remember every detail of it, though it clearly hadn't happened since I was still alive, still here. Was it just a terrible nightmare, like the rest of the trip?

I wrapped my arms around my chest and shivered. Falling like that was something I never wanted to experience again. I pulled the blankets up around my face and suppressed the urge to scream. "Jessica, don't ever let me go skydiving, okay?" I slid back into bed and closed my eyes.

Jessica rested her brush down on the counter. "Are you just going to sit in that bed all day again? God, Autumn, just take that medicine for seasickness. Can't you try to enjoy this vacation just a little? I want you to have some good memories, because God knows when we'll ever get away together again."

My eyes shot open. Was she serious? I wished I'd spent the cruise in bed. I'd be a lot better off. More normal. Less psychotic. Hopefully healthy.

I snuck a peek at my body. No bruises. I glanced at my pillow. No hair.

Thank God.

"Um, sorry Jessica. I'm just…I'm fine. I'll get out today. Promise. I feel much better."

She smiled. "Good. Glad to hear. You've missed so much the past few days."

Ha. I wish. "What about Joey and Marcus?" I asked.

"What about them?"

I didn't know what to ask. Was I carrying one of their babies? Engaged or married to one of them? "Have you seen them much this trip?"

She shook her head. "Marcus spends all his time with his family reunion people. Joey and I hung out a few times and went to the comedy show last night together. He's been asking about you a lot, but that's no surprise. Why?"

I shrugged. "Just wondered."

She picked up her lip gloss and tossed it in her beach bag. "Well, I'm going to enjoy this weather and our last day. Come on out when you're ready."

I started climbing out of bed. "Hold up, Jessica. I'll come with you if you wait for me."

She stopped and smiled. "Cool. You got it."

"Give me twenty minutes." I rummaged through my clothes and picked out a hot-pink tankini and white terrycloth cover-up. I stopped right before I went into the bathroom. "Jessica?"

"Hmm?"

"I'm sorry."

She stared at me with confusion splashed on her face. "For what?"

I looked at the floor. "For everything." For an awkward moment, we stood there like strangers unsure of each other.

"Were you drinking last night?" she asked. But when I glanced at her, a smile spread across her face even as she tried to look mad.

I chuckled. "No, but maybe you can slip me one of your drinks to loosen me up, huh?"

I hopped in the shower while Jessica read the latest issue of *People* magazine. The warm water pulsating on my face felt like fingers beating some sense into me. I knew I needed it.

I got ready in fifteen minutes and followed Jessica to the pool deck, wondering what horrible reality awaited me. Had I escaped them, or had one of them followed me out of the Triangle?

We chose chairs that were out of the way of the crowds but still in the sun. I broke out the book of conspiracy theories about the Bermuda Triangle and kept reading, looking for any clues about what might happen next. The giant gas bubble theory made me laugh and reminded me of Nisha. Large amounts of methane gas released from the ocean floor supposedly made the water unable to hold up boats? Really? The ocean floor was farting people to death? Give me a break.

Jessica worked on a crossword puzzle next to me. The calm turquoise ocean rocked tiny waves all around us. The clear sky held the sun in the perfect position to warm me.

I finally felt some sense of relief from the past few days. I put the book down and tapped Jessica on the shoulder. "Remember when you used to do my hair?"

She stuffed the pencil behind her ear and smiled. "Sure. Why?"

I shrugged. "I just wanted to say thanks for all that time you spent helping me. You were a good sister, Jess. Are a good sister, I mean."

Her smiled widened. "I knew that. It's about damn time you figured it out!"

First step is always admitting there's a problem, right? Or was it admitting that I was the problem…

I stuck my tongue out at her and leaned back into my chair. She put her puzzle down and closed her eyes.

A tear slid down my cheek. Strength began building up inside me. Dad had told me nothing was my fault. I needed to confirm that when I got home before I could believe it. What if the Triangle was just messing with me? I considered 'fessing up to Jessica. I peeked at her in the chair next to me. Her sunglasses sat on her nose, sliding down the sweaty slope. Her mouth hung open. Drool slid down her chin.

I wiped the tear with the back of my hand and stared out over the ocean.

"Hi, Autumn. Mind if I sit?"

I turned to see Joey pointing to an empty chair next to me. I nodded and motioned toward the seat.

His eyes widened as he sat. A grin settled over his tanned face. "Thanks. How's your trip going?"

I shook my head. Were things normal now? How would I even know? Jessica seemed more like herself today. No one tried to claim I was their girlfriend. Yet. But Jessica said we'd left Bermuda behind last night, so maybe, just maybe, the craziness was over.

"Words cannot describe what I've been through over the past few days. You?"

He chuckled. "All right, I guess. My grandparents are nice, but they're old and not interested in anything I want to do. I hung out with Jessica a bit, but mostly I've been at the pool." He glanced at the ground. "I was hoping to spend a little time with you, too."

Yeah, I figured. Obviously, he wasn't aware of my Twilight Zone experience, because I'd spent plenty of time with him. My thoughts shuffled back to yesterday when I'd realized I had feelings for Joey. Looking at him now, bare-chested and tan, with a pair of cut-off jeans shorts and flip-flops, I felt them again. I wasn't ready to admit it to him, but I couldn't deny it to myself any longer.

I sighed, warring with myself over whether or not to let him into my life. My real life.

Here goes nothing. "Want to get something to eat?"

His smile threatened to swallow his face, it was so big. "Yes! Burgers? No, you like pizza. Pizza and hot dogs. I can get us—"

I put my hand up to stop him. "Don't try so hard, okay?" I put my book away. "Burgers sound good. Let's go."

We walked over to the Burger Bar and ordered cheeseburgers and fries. We stood in awkward silence as we waited for our food, glancing around at the people scattered all over the place. For once, he wasn't trying to pursue me. And for once, I wasn't running from him.

Man, that Triangle messed things up good. Or did it fix things? I had no clue.

"I'm going to get a table." I pointed over my shoulder toward the bistro tables with their colorful umbrellas. "I'll get some ketchup, too."

"Okay. I'll bring the burgers when they're done."

I grabbed salt, napkins, and ketchup and found an unoccupied table. I sat down and looked up just in time to see Marcus approaching.

"Hey there." The sight of him sped up my pulse. His bare chest was even more muscled than Joey's. Wearing wet swim trunks, with a towel thrown over his shoulder, he looked like he just stepped out of an ad for men's cologne.

I threw a glance toward the Burger Bar. Joey still waited for our lunch with his back to me.

"Hi, Marcus. Enjoying your trip?"

"More so now." He reached out for the chair across from me. "I'd been hoping to spend more time with you, Rayne, but you were stuck in that cabin with your seasickness. You feeling better today?"

"That seat's taken," I said.

He rested his hand on the back of Joey's chair. "Oh? By whom?"

Another voice answered. "Me."

Marcus and I turned to see Joey heading toward us with two plates in his hands.

Marcus looked at him, then back at me. "You're kidding. Him?"

"Yeah," Joey answered him. "Me."

He set the plates down in front of me and the empty chair, then stood in front of Marcus, waiting for him to move so he could sit.

Ugh. Not this shit again. "Marcus, let him sit, please."

Marcus smirked at Joey. "Having your girl fight for you, eh? Pretty cool, man."

I stood up. "Marcus, please. I asked Joey to have lunch with me. So, if you don't mind, would you leave and let us eat?"

Marcus winked at me. "Only if you agree to have dinner with me later."

The look Joey gave him could've frozen a lion in the jungle. "You need to learn some respect, little man. She asked you to leave." He pointed away from the table. "Show a little consideration and get going."

Marcus laughed. "Yeah, sure, buddy. You gonna help me out of here?"

Joey put a hand on Marcus's shoulder. "If I have to, I will."

So much for a nice last day. I shoved my chair into the person behind me and headed toward the bar, ignoring their testosterone-fueled competition. As I waited for my drink, someone tapped my shoulder.

I jumped and turned around to see Marcus smoldering at me. "Hey. Sorry about that. It's just…" He lowered his head and sighed. "I really like you. And if you go out with Joey, you'll end up some motorhead's girl. I could offer you so much more than he can."

I frowned at him. If only he'd known what I had seen of him these past few days. I think I knew just what he had to offer.

The bartender slid my iced tea across the counter. I reached for it, but Marcus grabbed it first. "Rayne, give me a chance. You deserve someone who can treat you like a queen."

I rolled my eyes. "Can I have my drink, please?"

I tried to grab my glass again, but he pulled it away from me. The playful smirk on his face made my stomach quiver.

"If you want it, come get it." He stepped around the side of the bar.

I crossed my arms over my chest. "Marcus, come on. Give it to me!" I followed him around the bar. He set my drink down, grabbed my arms, and pulled me to him.

"Are you ready for it, Rayne? I've been waiting for this moment."

I opened my mouth to protest, but Marcus's mouth met mine and stifled the sound. He kissed me gently at first, then harder, pressing me against the wall, making escape impossible. I fought against him, but he was too strong for me. The struggle made my bathing suit top ride up, leaving more skin exposed than I'd intended.

He pulled away from my face and smiled. "That's what you're missing." His body held mine hostage. "And it only gets better, babe."

With my body still pinned, all I had was my voice. I sounded out every single word so he wouldn't misunderstand. "Get. The. Fuck. Off. Me!" If I'd had more leverage, I would've headbutted the bastard.

"Come on, Rayne. Give me a chance. I've had my eye on you for a while." He leaned in to kiss me again.

I turned my head to the side in time to see Joey walking past with drinks in both hands. Our eyes connected. I didn't have to speak; he knew I needed him.

He dropped the drinks. Ice and brown liquid sprayed some kids playing on the ground. One of them yelped.

Joey was next to us in a heartbeat.

"Get off of her!" He grabbed Marcus by the arm and pulled him back. Marcus stumbled and caught himself on the edge of the stairs.

I gasped for breath. I didn't realize how hard he'd been pushing to hold me in place. With my boobs practically giving everyone a free show, I yanked the edge of my top down.

Before Marcus could stabilize himself, I pushed Joey out of the way, pulled my arm back, and punched Marcus in the mouth with every muscle I had. He fell to the ground and clapped a hand over his mouth. "Don't you ever touch me again!" I screamed. I shook out the sting that was flooding my fist.

He rubbed his quickly-reddening lip and glanced at the other passengers. "I'm sorry. Geez, Rayne, you didn't have to hit me. "

I leaned in to his face. "Next time, it won't be your face I'm aiming for. You'll be impotent for a month." I straightened up and grabbed Joey's hand. "Let's get out of here."

I led him to my chair by Jessica and sat down. My hands shook as I tried to reclaim my sense of calm.

Joey sat next to me and took both my hands in his. "I'm so sorry he did that to you. Are you okay?"

I looked at his hands around mine. They shook from my shaking. "I never hit anyone before." I let out a little laugh, shocked at my actions. "Damn, it hurts!"

He gave my hands a squeeze, steadying them and rubbing my knuckles. "You could've fooled me. You dropped him! Way to go. I'm still sorry, though. I should have stopped him from following you. Can I get you some ice for your hand?"

I took a few deep breaths. "Could you just get me another iced tea and my burger, please? I'm still hungry."

He smiled and released my hands. "Sure. Be right back."

I checked out my boxing hand as he walked away. Little areas of purple and red popped up here and there. Ugh, I hoped nothing was broken. I flexed my fingers and they all seemed to work, but they felt tight and swollen. "Hey Joey, yeah. Bring that ice for my hand too, please."

Jessica stirred and sat up. "Hey, Raynie. What's going on?" Her voice drawled with sleep as she wiped her chin with the back of her hand.

I crossed my arms over my chest. "Same old shit."

My right hand throbbed. I rubbed it with my other hand and looked for Joey.

He juggled two glasses of iced tea and a steaming plate of fries. I hopped up and took the fries with my left hand, carrying them to the table we'd occupied before Marcus decided to ruin our day with his bullshit. Our burgers were still there, beckoning me to take a bite.

I looked toward the bar for Marcus. The ice from the tea Joey had dropped was melting into little glistening puddles near the bar, but Marcus was gone.

"I'll go get that ice for you." Joey ran to the bar before I could say anything.

I suddenly remembered what Joey had said when the cruise started. When he came back a minute later, I took the cup of ice and plunged in as much of my hand as could fit. "Can I ask you something?"

He nodded. "Anything."

"When we got on the ship, you said you and Marcus were brothers, yet you guys seem to hate each other. What's the deal?"

His face darkened. He picked up his burger and took an angry bite, chewing for a minute before answering.

I snapped my fingers in front of him. "Joey? You going to tell me?"

He shrugged. "Um, do you know that my mom's sick?"

I nodded.

"Okay. Marcus's dad was married to my mom when she was young. They had Marcus, but his dad cheated on my mom and left her for the other woman. A rich woman. He lied to the judge and said my mom was a jobless drunk and a bad mother, so he could get custody of Marcus, then his wife adopted Marcus." He took a long drag on his straw, then held the icy glass against his forehead. "My mom married my dad a year later, but my dad left after my twin brothers were born. Anyway, Marcus knows my mom—our mom—is sick. She's his real mom and he doesn't care or help her at all. His dad has lots of money, but won't help with any of her medical bills and never paid her any of the money he was supposed to in the divorce." He popped a fry into his mouth. "She doesn't have the money to get a lawyer to fight him on it, so he just gets away with it. I hate men who won't step up. Marcus and his dad, they're both assholes. They're both the same."

I stared at Joey. This guy that I'd known and avoided for six months was nothing like the weak, annoying, high-school geek I'd believed him to be. He was kind, compassionate, caring, loyal, and sweet. And he wasn't weak. He just picked his battles and protected his side with fierce conviction.

In short, he was the perfect guy for me.

Eighteen

After lunch, Joey and I returned to the lounge chairs to soak up some sun. He rubbed sunscreen on my back, refilled my glass whenever it was half-empty, and gently sprayed my arms and legs with water as the sun attempted to cook my skin.

As the sun slid lower and lower, Joey fell asleep. I stared at him for a long time. His dark hair glistened in the sun. His Italian skin soaked up the rays, giving him an even, perfect tan. He looked boyish and innocent as he slept. The definition in his muscles proved he was much more than a boy.

I closed my eyes, struggling with my thoughts. I didn't want a relationship. Not now, not when I was so close to eighteen and getting away. Yet Joey's loyalty to his friends and family, his kind heart, and his obvious feelings for me left me confused.

Since we were out of the Triangle, I assumed this was the real him. But when I thought about it, he had been just as sweet in the Triangle.

He would make a great boyfriend, in either place.

Did I deserve him? Now that I knew how I felt about him, I had to wonder—did I want to taint his life with the toxin I spread to everyone I cared about? He didn't need that. He had enough going on in his life. If I let him in, I would only make him suffer more.

I opened my eyes to look at him again. His head was turned toward me, his eyes now wide open.

He grinned. "What?"

I shook my head, my lips curving into a smile. "Nothing, Joey."

He stretched out, his toes fanning out in front of him. "I had a nice nap." He pulled his eyes away from me and looked at the pool. Most of the swimmers had gone. The water sat cool and inviting, and best of all, almost deserted. He looked back at me and tilted his head toward the pool. "Wanna go for a dip?"

I took a deep breath and sighed. I started this cruise in the pool with Marcus. I might as well end it in the pool with Joey.

"Sure."

He got up first, then held out a hand to help me.

When I stood, I kept his hand in mine. We played in the water for hours, splashing, swimming, laughing. When we were both so tired we could barely stand, he walked me to my cabin door.

"Autumn, I'm so glad we spent some time together. Maybe we can hang out after the cruise." With a shaking finger, he brushed a wet strand of hair out of my eyes.

I reached up on my tiptoes and kissed his cheek. "Maybe." I then turned and disappeared into the safety of my cabin.

I woke up happy for the first time in years.

Instead of ocean and sky out our cabin window, I saw only tall buildings, blacktop, and smokestacks. I turned my head to see Jessica sleeping on the couch. Her face was covered with her hair. Her red arms showed where the sun had triumphed over her sunscreen.

Our carry-ons were waiting by the door. If Jersey was looking back at me through the window, then the Bermuda Triangle was behind me.

The cruise was over. Thank God. I almost jumped out of bed and kissed the floor.

I called over to Jessica. "Hey, get up. We have to leave today. I think I forgot to pack my big suitcase."

She stretched and yawned, then looked at me. "We packed last night and left our luggage out, just like we were supposed to. You don't sound like you're awake yet," she said in a sleepy voice.

I blinked a few times and tried to remember the night before. I had no recollection of packing. I didn't even remember getting into bed. The last thing I remembered was hanging out with Joey.

I got out of bed and quickly dressed. "I'll be glad to get away from all this Joey and Marcus crap. The way they kept fighting over me was so middle school."

She laughed. "That's pretty cool, huh? Two guys fighting over you. Wish that would happen to me. I spent the day relaxing yesterday." She got up and pulled on white shorts and a black tank top. "I'm glad we got some sun in. The cruise was fantastic. For me, anyway."

I leveled my eyes at her. "Jessica, did you notice anything different the past few days? Like things not being what they are at home?"

She smiled. "Yes, I did. I noticed the sun, the sand, the breeze, the air—everything was better than in Jersey. Did you notice it?"

I slumped back down on the bed. I raised my arm to inspect it. No needle marks. Relief flooded every cell in my body. I felt my hair. Full, thick, and on my head. Jessica seemed normal, too. No pregnant belly. Maybe everything else was back to normal. No baby supplies littered the cabin floor. No notes from guys claiming me as theirs.

But that would mean Dad was still gone, and Mom was still sick.

Despite that, I almost cried.

Damn. Couldn't I have woken up to everything being perfect?

Jessica watched me slump back into bed. "Come on, Autumn, we have to eat quick before we get off the ship. Get up and get moving." She disappeared into the bathroom. "Breakfast is only at the buffet this morning."

We went to breakfast, filled our plates with our last taste of the ship's gourmet cooking, and sat by the entrance. I watched for Joey and Marcus, scanning each person who walked through the doors. I was halfway done with my ham and cheddar omelet when I caught a glimpse of Joey walking in with his grandparents from dinner that first night on the cruise.

Joey saw me and waved. I smiled and waved back. He looked good. Rested and happy. Why couldn't my trip through the Triangle have been like his?

Marcus came in a few minutes later with a big group of people, all wearing their "McKenna Family Reunion" shirts. He didn't notice me, but I noticed he had his arm around a short, pretty girl. They looked blissed out.

I guess he'd had fun, too.

Long red hair caught my eye by the door. Dr. Hardy stood just inside, arms lightly crossed over her chest, smiling at me.

I gave her a quick nod. She kept her gaze on me for a few seconds, nodded back, then slipped out the door.

I rose from my chair. "Jessica, I'll be right back. I have to go see someone for a minute." I rushed to the door and inspected the hall. Dr. Hardy was nowhere to be seen. I jogged down to the infirmary, but it was closed.

I'd find a way to talk to her. Maybe even help her since she'd said she was stuck in the Triangle.

Unless…she was a part of the Triangle like the cancer and my dad, but wasn't real. How would I talk to her if that was the case?

I returned to breakfast and looked at Jessica. She ate in silence with a book in her hand.

"Jessica?"

"Hmm?" She didn't look up.

"I'm glad we're home."

She dropped the book and smiled. "I hope you'll remember that when we actually get back to the apartment, and will stop giving me such a hard time. What do you say?"

"That depends." I placed my hands on my hips. "Are you going to keep giving me a hard time? It works both ways."

She laughed. "You're right. I'm glad we're home. I missed your usual attitude. Things seemed a bit odd on this ship, don't you think?"

I laughed and almost spit out my milk. "Odd" didn't even begin to cover it.

"You know, I can't believe Joey was sitting at our table. On a ship this big, what were the chances of that happening?" I laughed, but then noticed Jessica was looking away. Her eyes refused to look at me.

"Jessica? Do you have something to tell me?" Watching her eyes shift around the room, I knew there was a secret to be told in there somewhere.

She shrugged. "Well…"

My eyes opened wide. "I knew it! You did arrange for them to sit with us, didn't you?"

She stared at the floor.

"Thanks a lot! I can't believe you." I tried to make my glare convincing, but failed. "I'm going out on the deck one last time. Next time, I make the dinner arrangements!" When the smile broke out across my face, I didn't want her to see it.

She looked at me with a mouth full of food. "Sorry. I was only trying to help. I knew you guys would be great together."

"Jessica, I told you and Nisha, I didn't want to get involved with anyone. You couldn't let it be. Now look what you did." I looked over my shoulder before continuing. "Something happened with Joey, even though I didn't want it to."

"Did you guys hook up?" I could hear the smile in her voice.

"No! Yes. I mean, I don't know." I rolled my eyes. "Everyone I care about ends up sick or dead, and I don't want to drag anyone down with me, especially a decent guy like Joey. I just have to get out of here before I cause anyone else any more pain. Especially him."

A warm hand on my shoulder made me jump. I turned around and found myself looking at Joey. His smile could have turned an ice planet into a sun.

I jumped up from my seat. My face blazing like a four-alarm fire, I ran out of the dining room.

I wasn't ready to tell Joey how I felt. I was still sorting through it myself. That he had heard me confessing to Jessica mortified me. But I couldn't take it back now. I'd just have to suck it up and face him at some point.

And that would be harder than anything I'd faced in the Bermuda Triangle.

I found a little hidden corner under the stairs and sat down, hugging my knees to my chest. I tucked my head down and closed my eyes. I wanted to think before I had this discussion with Joey. I wanted to be prepared and do everything right this time.

I wasn't ready.

I heard slow footsteps coming toward me. Someone touched the back of my hair. I knew who it was.

"Mind if I sit?" Joey asked.

I nodded toward the space to my right.

I wrapped my hands tighter around my knees and put my head down as he sat next to me. "By the way, why didn't you tell me you were going on the cruise with your grandparents?"

"Because I didn't want you not to go because of me."

"Did you know Marcus was going?" I asked.

"Yeah. He goes with his rich family every year. I think my grandparents were hoping we could get to know each other, but you know how that went. He doesn't care about our mom or anyone else from her family." He shrugged. "You know, if he touches you again, you come to me. I can handle him, and I'll make sure he never handles you again."

"Didn't you notice my fist handling him?" I asked. "I can take care of myself, Joey. I don't need a guy doing it for me."

He chuckled. "Yeah, I noticed. I was proud of you. I've wanted to do that myself for a long time." His eyes avoided mine as he watched a seagull glide by. "Autumn, are we past the point where you pretend I don't exist?"

"I'm sorry, Joey. I just don't think I'm right for you." Didn't he know that everyone I loved got hurt? If I fell for him now, I may as well reserve the hospital bed next to Mom for him. Or the grave plot next to Dad. "I'm not worth the hassle you'll suffer through."

He sighed. "Why don't you let me decide what's worth fighting for and what isn't?"

I rolled my eyes and looked away. The sun was blocked by dark clouds. A cool breeze came in off the water, filling the air with the scent of salt and fish. I shivered.

"Are you cold?"

I shivered again but didn't answer. He closed the tiny space between us and put his arm around my shoulders. The minute he touched me, sparks flew through me. My feelings for him were changing so fast, I felt like I needed a seatbelt to strap myself into my life.

When he spoke next, his voice was husky. "You okay?"

I drew in a deep breath and sighed. "Fine. Thanks for warming me up."

He rubbed my shoulder, then tucked my head into his firm chest. "I know you're going through a rough time, and I can't imagine how hard things must be for you. But I want you to know that I'm here for you if you need anything. It'll all work out in the end, I'm sure. You're gonna be okay."

I wondered if he would think I was nuts if I asked about the ship. I played with the lace of my sneaker. "Thanks, Joey. Did you notice anything strange on the ship while we were in Bermuda?"

"What do you mean by strange?"

"Like, you know, things being different than what they really are." I added hesitantly, "Like, alternate reality sort of stuff?"

He looked up at the sky, which seemed to be getting darker by the minute, then shook his head. "No. I was kind of bored with my grandparents, but other than that, I had hoped to spend more time with you." His cheeks turned red at his words. "Why do you ask?"

"Never mind." I pushed him away and stood up. "I have to go. Jessica is going to be looking for me to disembark." I started climbing up the stairs. I turned back to him to say something and slipped. He caught me in his strong arms and helped me right myself.

I couldn't let go of him. I squeezed tighter, drawing strength from his strength. He was so warm, and his arms around me felt better than I wanted them to. All of my emotions clung to me like bacteria. I wanted to jump into the ocean and scrub my body until every bad thing got washed away.

The control over my emotions I fought so hard to keep was crumbling. Fast.

I finally found it in me to pull away. "Thanks again. You keep saving me, Joey."

He lifted my chin with his finger until I was forced to look at him. Staring into his dark eyes drew me to him like a cat to catnip. I threw my arms around him, burying my face in his neck. He wound his arms around me and held me tight. I wanted to be a part of his life, but I didn't want to bring him any more misery. His life was hard enough without me.

I took a deep breath. When I spoke, I couldn't look him in the eye. "I've been through too much for me to handle any more. I'm just…done. I'm trying. But I don't know how to handle everything. I don't know what I want or need anymore."

He stared out over the water. "Autumn, I knew the day I met you that you needed a guy who would treat you right for once. I also knew it would take you a while to figure it out." He chuckled. "Good thing I'm a patient guy, huh?" He looked down at me. "I've liked you for a long time. You know that. If we went to high school together, I would've followed you around the halls like a lost puppy." He smiled at my now tear-streaked face and wiped a fresh tear away with his thumb. "I have a confession to make."

I peeked up at him, not sure I wanted to hear the confession. I opened my mouth to speak, but he put his finger over my lips.

"It's nothing weird, don't worry." He let a nervous laugh slip as he spoke. "Just don't be mad at me, okay?"

I motioned with my hand for him to continue.

He looked down at his feet. "My grandparents didn't just surprise me with this cruise. I, um, asked to be on this ship because I knew you were going to be here." He sneaked a sideways glance at me. When I didn't speak, he squeezed my shoulder. "Are you mad?"

I turned to face him and sighed. "No." His face relaxed at my words. I gazed into his eyes. He stared back with the most honest, trusting expression I had ever seen. I knew with Joey that nothing was fake.

He was the real deal.

The world around me disappeared. It was just me and him. Staring into his eyes, I realized why I pushed against him so hard. I was just afraid of getting my delicate heart broken any worse than it already was. It was about one fracture line away from breaking into pieces and giving up on me.

Before my brain could stop my body, I reached up on my toes toward him. He bent down and brushed his lips over mine. Butterflies woke up in my stomach as his touch made my entire body tingle. I wound my arms around his neck and pulled him to me, molding my body and mouth to his. His tongue explored my mouth, his hands wrapped around my waist, pulling me to him. I clung to him like my life depended on it. Who knew, maybe it did.

He bowed my body closer to his. I dropped my hands from his neck and let them brush along his arms, gripping his biceps. He moaned and lifted me up off the ground as he kissed me. Tears ran down my face as my brain tried to stop my body from reacting. The realization of how much I needed him and how much I wanted him kept me clinging to his body.

He seated me on the three-foot high rail. I wrapped my legs around his waist and leaned back as he kissed my neck, holding the ledge tight so I didn't fall. "Babe, I've waited so long for this," he whispered in my ear.

His words snapped me out of the spell I'd been under. I pushed him away gently and slipped off the rail to stand on my own. "Stop. Please."

He was breathless. "What's wrong? I just—"

The disappointment on his face worsened my guilt. I couldn't take it. "Joey, I'm broken. You can't fix me like you fix cars. I really wish you could, but—"

"Autumn, we're so good for each other. Please, don't push me away now." He reached for me but I took a step back. "Let me help you. I… want you, Autumn. More than anything I've ever wanted."

I backed away from him. He was about to join everyone else who was cursed by knowing me. I didn't want that to happen to him.

"Don't do this. Don't shut me out." He stepped toward me, his hands reaching. "Let me in, Autumn." He stopped walking as I backed up, and he held his hands out in surrender. Our eyes were locked on each other.

"I need some time. Please." I took another step backward. "I'm just starting to understand things, and I finally feel like my life's getting better. Give me some space, Joey. That's all I ask. I think there's room in my life for you, but I want to be sure before I rush into anything. Understand?"

I backed up another step as he stood frozen, probably afraid I'd bolt if he came any closer. I wanted to let him in. I really did. But could my fragile heart handle it?

Joey would be the only one I could trust not to break it.

I smiled and closed my eyes as I realized that, yes, I would let him in.

"Autumn, watch out!"

I stumbled over something on the ground behind me. He jumped to grab me, but I twisted away from him as I fell. His hands grabbed for me, but they only succeeded in pushing me further.

I toppled over the edge of the rail.

I scratched and clawed to grab something, anything to hold on to, but only air passed through my fingers. Finally, things were coming together and my life didn't suck. Was the Triangle doing this to claim me, angry that I'd made it out in better shape than I was in when I entered?

As I plummeted toward the dark water below, the last thing I heard was my own voice screaming his name.

Nineteen

I remembered flashing red and blue lights and voices of people both familiar and unfamiliar swirling through my head. The sensation of my body floating through the air yet being tightly restrained didn't make sense to me. Sudden bright lights and the smell of alcohol forced my face into a contorted grimace. My cold, wet body shivered uncontrollably. I imagined this was what it must feel like to be a pickle in the fridge.

A sharp stab in my hand introduced warm liquid that toned everything down to a dull blur. Someone wrapped me in thick, wool blankets. As I faded, the light dimmed. The comfort and warmth injected into me turned into discomfort and coolness.

And then, darkness. Pain. Noise. Hunger. Thirst.

The sensations were so strong, it seemed like I'd never felt them before. I couldn't open my eyes. Then I heard Joey plead, "Autumn?"

I still couldn't open my eyes, but I reached out my hand. A warm, rough hand grabbed it. I smelled motor oil and gasoline and would have known who it was even without a voice attached.

"Joey?" My voice came out all wrong. It sounded like I'd smoked a whole pack of cigarettes in five minutes.

"Yeah, baby, it's Joey. Are you okay? Are you in pain? I'm so sorry!" A whimper escaped from him.

"Joey, stop asking her so many questions. Let her wake up first. The doctor said she should take it easy." Jessica's strained voice echoed in my other ear.

Oh, no. Doctor? Did the cancer follow me out of the Triangle? I knew it. I was done.

"Jessica?" I squinted one eye at her. "Do I still have cancer?"

"No, you don't have cancer. You fell. Remember?" She cried quietly. "Oh, Autumn! I'm so sorry! Oh God, I thought you were dead!"

"What day is it? How long have I've been here?"

"It's Saturday, June twenty-sixth. You fell yesterday."

I reached for her hand, and she took mine in hers. Jessica and Joey each held one of my hands, both of them crying now.

"It's okay, guys," I croaked. My throat hurt, but I didn't know why. A salty taste on my tongue dug up a memory of falling into the deep, dark ocean.

I heard someone come into the room. A cold hand checked my pulse. "Okay everyone, let's let Autumn get some rest. You can come back tomorrow during visiting hours."

I released the hands that held mine and fell into a dreamless sleep. The doctor came in some time after it was dark, checked me out, and told me I would be just fine. Then he teased me about diving off the ship when I should have used the diving board in the pool.

Jessica came to my room with a huge stuffed bear the minute visiting hours started the next day. Her hair was a mess, and her eyes were swollen and puffy. Dark circles sat under each eye. I knew she hadn't slept much the night before.

I smiled at her. She ran to my bedside and hugged me tight, tears leaking out of her eyes.

"I'm—"

"It's okay, Jessica. It was an accident." I tugged her arm so she would join me on the bed and then rubbed her back. "Joey tried to save me. The doctor came in last night and said I was going to be fine."

She nodded, her face still buried in my neck.

I hugged her hard. "Thank you. For taking care of me when Mom couldn't. And for putting up with me. I'm better now, and I'll make it up to you."

"You don't have to. I had no problem taking care of you. Did I wish you were nicer to me? Maybe." She laughed. "But no matter what, I'm not about to risk losing you. Mom and Dad were enough for me to handle. If anything happened to you, I would lose my mind. All we have is each other."

I looked at her, my eyes threatening to tear up. We smiled at each other and hugged again.

After a minute, I pushed her away. "Dad's death and Mom's accident have been really hard for me to accept—so hard that I've been pushing you away because I didn't think I could handle it if I lost you, too. I'm sorry, Jessica."

"I know it's hard. I guess we haven't really talked about it much."

"I need to know something. Do you know how Dad died, and what happened to Mom?"

She pulled away and looked at me. Concern colored her face. "Why? Do you have amnesia? Oh God, we should call the doctor—"

I put my hand up. "Calm down. I don't have amnesia, I just never knew more than that they were both in car accidents. I guess I was afraid to know all the details, so I shut it out."

She drew in a deep breath and sighed. "Dad was killed by a drunk driver. The guy crossed the middle of the road and hit him head-on."

Not my fault. I closed my eyes and savored the feeling. "And what about Mom? What happened to her?" I opened my eyes and stared at Jessica, trying hard to keep my face unreadable.

"It was the truck driver's fault. He jackknifed because he braked too hard and was going too fast."

"You sure it wasn't because Mom had car trouble or something?"

Jessica shook her head. "Mom had some car trouble that morning, so she took the car to the mechanic. She called to tell me she got it fixed. I was going to meet her for lunch on my break from work, then there was that terrible accident on Route Nine." Tears began streaming down her face, but she pressed on. "It was really bad, but she was alive, so they brought her here. You know the rest." She searched my face and touched my cheek. "Why are you asking these questions now?"

I stared out the window. "You'll think I'm nuts if I tell you."

She squeezed my arm. "No I won't."

I took a deep breath. "Do you remember me telling you on the ship that I…um…that I saw Dad?"

She shook her head. "Like in a dream? What happened?" She kept her hand on my arm, rubbing it like Mom used to do when I was upset.

"Well, um, not a dream, but maybe more like a ghost or an angel…" I trailed off, still not sure how much she would believe. What if she took me to the psychiatric unit?

"Go on, Autumn. Tell me."

I kept my eyes on the world outside the window. "While we were in the Bermuda Triangle, I saw Dad. I didn't know if it was a dream or if it was real, but it affected me." I sighed and turned to look at her.

"I would've given anything to see him one more time," she said, sounding a bit jealous.

I nodded. "It was amazing." Jessica focused on my eyes as I spoke. "The reason I didn't want to go back to school was because I was saving my money to get away. I look around this area, and I'm reminded every day of Mom, or Dad, or something that I did to hurt someone. I thought leaving would make everything go away, but I'm not so sure anymore. I might go back. Seeing and talking to Dad helped me through stuff." I reached up to brush the wetness off my cheeks. "You understand, right?"

"I do. And I'm glad. I'd hoped you would change your mind. Running away never solves anything, Autumn."

"I sorta noticed. Even on a cruise ship, my problems found a way to follow me."

I knew I only had seconds to speak before the floodgates opened. "All this time, I thought both of their accidents were because of me. I thought everything was my fault." And that was it. I burst into tears that flowed in rivers. I cried so hard my lungs hurt, but I couldn't stop. All the guilt over Dad, the guilt and self-hatred over Mom—it poured out of me like a dam finally giving way.

The whole time I cried, Jessica held me. She rocked me, stroked my hair, rubbed my back. And that only made it worse. Because I'd given her hell half the time, and she'd done nothing but try to help me.

When the tears dried up, I was too exhausted to keep my eyes open.

"Jessica, so much happened to me on that ship. I went through some crazy stuff. Joey found me while we were at the port. I was sort of freaking out. Then, while he was talking to me and holding me as I cried, I just realized…"

"That you like Joey," she finished. "I'm so glad. Joey is such a nice guy. You could use someone like that to treat you right. See, I knew what I was doing when I pushed you guys together!" She winked at me and smiled.

I backtracked a bit. "I never said I was happy that you pushed us together." But when she smirked at me, I knew she knew how I felt. I tried to stop the smile spreading across my face, but it lit up without my consent. "But I do like him. I never planned on that happening." I laughed, and she chuckled. "He seemed so needy at first, you know? Calling me, leaving things for me at work, texting me, showing up at our house…"

"See, Autumn? People aren't always what they seem. Now, visiting hours are over, and I've got your cat to go home to and feed, and then I need to get ready. Andy is taking me out for dinner tonight."

"Andy?"

She grinned. "I met him on the ship. He works at the hospital across town. We hung out a few times, and he asked me for my number."

I recalled Marcus saying on the ship that Jessica's husband, Andy, had died of melanoma before their baby was born. I hoped that wasn't prophetic. "Does he have skin cancer?"

She wrinkled her brows. "Why would you ask that?"

I shook my head. "Never mind. Just thinking about skin cancer after all that sun on the cruise."

"If we get to know each other better, I'll ask him. Now, you just rest and take it easy."

I grabbed her hand and squeezed. "Thanks, Jessica. You're the best. Kiss Sleepy for me when you get home."

I woke up, alone and hungry, a long time later. I wondered where Jessica had gone. I gazed up at the bear she'd brought and smiled.

The soft tinkling of bells made me turn my head to my right. The biggest, most colorful bouquet of helium balloons I'd ever seen sat next to me on my bedside table, anchored with tiny silver bells. A card stuck out from the shiny cluster.

I pulled it out and opened it. When I read it, it confused me. The only words on the card said, "Turn around."

I swung my head to the left. Joey stood next to my bed in a cruise logo T-shirt and jeans. He smiled at me and held a single balloon that said, "I'm yours."

I motioned for him to come sit with me. He dragged a chair over to the side of the bed and sat down, tying the balloon string to my IV pole.

His bottom lip quivered. "I thought…when you fell…I tried to catch you…" He put his head down on the edge of my bed and covered it with his hands.

I stroked his hair. "Joey, it was an accident. Stop blaming yourself." If I knew anything, I knew how much of a burden false guilt was. He nodded, but kept his head down.

I pulled his hands away from his head and held them. "By the way, thank you."

He sniffled. "For what?"

"For saving my life. If you weren't there, I'm sure I would've drowned."

He lifted his head, his eyes filled with anger. "No. If I wasn't there, you never would've backed away from me and fallen. I'm so sorry." Another tear slipped down his cheek.

"Joey, this is not your fault, you hear me? You called for help the instant I fell and got the crew to fish me out. You were always nice to me, even when I was so mean to you. I don't understand why you put up with me."

He chuckled. "I can tell you why. Your mom came in to get her car fixed at the shop. I actually think it was the day before she had that accident, or even the day it happened, now that I think of it. I fixed her car. And when I opened the door to drive it into the shop, I saw she had a picture on her passenger seat." He smiled at the memory. "When your mom came to pick up the car, I couldn't help but comment on the picture. She said, 'That's my beautiful daughter, Autumn. My girls are my life.' Then she thanked me for fixing her car and left."

I couldn't tear my eyes away from him. "Then she had the accident—"

"That day. I couldn't stop thinking about you. You walked into the shop a few weeks later, looking for a job. I told Colin he had to hire you." He laughed. "Of course, I didn't know you had such an attitude problem back then, but I knew about what had happened to your mom. I have a sick mom, too. I saw how hard it was for you."

My face burned. Here he was, a total stranger, realizing how hard my life was, and I'd never noticed how much he was going through.

He pursed his lips. "I wanted to be friends, but I never expected to fall for you." His cheeks reddened. "But who could blame me? You're a beautiful girl, Autumn."

I pulled him to me and slipped my arms around his neck. He hesitated, then wrapped his arms around me and held me tight. I whispered in his ear. "Thanks. I owe you my life."

He shivered.

"Come here. Climb in here with me." I moved over on the bed and pulled the blanket back, making room for him.

He glanced at the door. "But what about the nurses? Won't they kick me out?"

"I'll tell them to leave you the hell alone." I smiled. "You know I will, right? Come on."

He lifted the covers and slid into the bed next to me. His body trembled, and I noticed his breathing increase. He always seemed nervous around me. I was nervous, too. It had been so long since I had allowed myself to feel anything for a guy. "There. Better?"

He nodded and glanced down at me. He kissed me so gently, I trembled. When he pulled away, I gazed into his eyes.

They reflected everything I wanted.

Jessica came back later, dressed in her nursing scrubs.

I sat up in bed. "Hey. Can you take me to see Mom? I have some things I want to tell her."

She pursed her lips. "Um, Autumn, no one really knows if a person in a coma can hear you. I mean, I believe they can, but we really don't know. Are you sure you want to go? I don't want you getting too upset after everything you've been through."

I nodded. "I have to talk to her. I know she'll hear me."

She glanced out into the hallway. "Okay, hold on. Let me go get a wheelchair." She left, coming back with a wheelchair a minute later. She locked the wheels and helped me ease into the seat.

I was on a floor near the ICU, so Mom was close. We only went a short distance when Jessica turned left into the noisy unit.

A young nurse carrying two jugs of white liquid looked at us and smiled. "Hey, Jessica, what's up?"

I kept my eyes on her as Jessica spoke. "I have a visitor for Isabel Taylor." She patted the top of my head. "Nadia, this is my sister, Autumn. She's a patient here, too."

"Hi, Autumn. Go ahead in, girls. You can talk to her. She can hear you."

Jessica pushed the chair toward Mom's room.

I peeked around the corner as we made our way to the door. A small plastic chair sat next to the bed. Monitors with digital numbers displayed her vital signs. Occasional beeps and chirps sounded throughout the small room, just like I'd remembered. "Get Well" cards papered the walls. Faded flowers drooped by the window, and I could see Jessica's handwriting on the little card sticking out of the center of the bouquet.

Nothing was from me.

"It's okay, Autumn. All that matters is that you're here now." Jessica noticed how I was eyeing the flowers. "Everyone works through these things differently. Don't worry about it."

She put her hand on my shoulder and wheeled me to Mom's side. I still couldn't look at Mom's face with Jessica around. I looked back at her and touched her hand. "Would you mind leaving me alone with Mom? I just... I need to talk to her alone."

"Sure." Jessica pushed the chair up to Mom's bed and locked the brakes. I waited until I heard Jessica close the door, leaving me alone with our mom, before I spoke.

I refused to look at her face. I concentrated instead on the wedding ring she still wore. She'd lost weight since the accident, so it hung loose on her finger.

I spoke to the ring. "Can't you get better? Please wake up. I'm sorry. I swear I didn't steal the car to hurt you. I never meant for this to happen. I need you, Mommy."

I reached out to take her hand, half-afraid to touch her delicate skin.

Then, for the first time in a half a year, I looked at her face, and really looked at her.

Big mistake. The months of being sick and on all kinds of tubes and medicine made her look like a bloated doll. Her eyes were closed, tubes came out of her mouth and arms, and she smelled like baby powder and pee. The tears ran down my cheeks before I could stop them.

It took me a minute to get myself together so I could speak. I cleared my swollen throat. "Hi Mom. It's me, Autumn."

Nothing else came easy. All the guilt over her accident, my fall, and seeing Dad just tied my tongue into knots. I wanted to say everything and nothing. I wanted to yell and scream and whisper and cry. How did I put all of that into words? There was no way.

I fought back the tears and continued. I owed her that much. "I'm sorry, Mom. So sorry for everything. I hope you can forgive me for being such a terrible person. I never wanted…I mean, I didn't know what would happen…I just, I'm sorry." I wiped my nose on the sleeve of my hospital gown. I looked at her face for signs of understanding, but she remained still.

"Mom, I don't know if you can hear me, but I think you can. I saw Dad. He's doing great. He explained everything to me. And I'm better now. And I want you to get better, too. I hope you can. And…I love you."

Jessica came back into the room, humming on the way in so I could hear her entering. "You almost ready? You have to get some blood drawn."

I wiped the tears away before she could see them. "Yeah, let's go. Bye, Mom." I reached out to touch her hair.

That's when I saw it—a single tear sliding down Mom's swollen cheek.

Twenty

The day I was released from the hospital, Nisha walked into my room at home with a stuffed cat and a box of pizza. The sight of her warmed my messed-up heart, forcing a grin out of me. "Well, well. You did this just to get out of working, right? Because now I'm stuck doing extra shifts, and the customers are driving me crazy, and—"

I threw my arms around her and squeezed as hard as I could.

"Can't breathe…can't breathe," she squeaked out.

I laughed and released her. She tossed the stuffed cat on my bed and flipped open the pizza box. "Take a slice. I'm sure you missed Tony's pizza almost as much as you missed me."

I pulled out a slice and stuffed half of it in my mouth.

It tasted like Take-Out Heaven.

She plopped down on my bed and eyed me. "You look a little too happy, Autumn. What's the deal?"

I shrugged. "What do you mean?"

She crossed her arms over her chest. "Come on, stop holding out on me. Spill. What happened on your trip?"

I told her everything that happened. I even told her about Dr. Hardy and seeing her photo in that Bermuda Triangle book. "I think she had a reason to be there." I leaned closer to her. "I think she was letting me know that, no matter what's wrong in my life, it could always be worse."

"So, what, you think she was, like, an angel?"

I lifted a shoulder. "Don't know. But as far as I'm concerned," I said, my voice shaking, "the Triangle saved me. It let me see my dad one more time. It showed me how I truly felt about Joey. And it let me see that my life wasn't so bad. You know what I mean?"

She grinned at me. "Yeah. I know what you mean. You're not only nuts, but it took a cruise through Hell to make you realize just how lucky you really are."

I giggled. "Ain't it the truth."

The phone rang, so I grabbed my cell and flipped it open. "Hello?"

The ringing continued. I blinked and realized it was the house phone. I dropped my cell and hurried into the kitchen, yanking the receiver off the wall. "Hello?"

"Hi, is Jessica there? This is Cara, her friend from the hospital. I need to speak to her. Right now."

"She's taking a nap, Cara, before she works the late shift."

"Wake her up. It's important."

I brought the cordless into Jessica's room and shook her shoulder. "Jessica, it's Cara. She said she has to speak to you right now."

She rolled over and ripped the phone from my hands, her eyes still shut. "Cara, what's wrong?"

Jessica opened her eyes, looked at me with shock and screamed, "Mom's awake!"

Despite the emotional excitement of the past week and the exhaustion that followed, I finally went back to work a couple days later. After lunch, Joey came over to my register at Shore Auto. "Hiya, babe. How's your mom?" He kissed my cheek.

"We had a long talk with the doctor, and Jessica understood a lot more of it than I did. They said it will be a long road to recovery. Her chances look pretty good, though." I beamed. "That night I visited, her nurse noticed some changes. Good changes. They started taking tubes and stuff out. Today, she opened her eyes and asked for us again."

He stroked my cheek. "I'm so glad for you guys. I hope she comes home soon."

I sighed. "I know. Me too."

A wicked gleam shot through his eyes. "Guess what I did while you were at lunch?"

"Tell me."

He leaned over the counter to whisper in my ear. "I changed Marcus's oil. He dropped off his car last night. Not his daddy's fancy car, but his old Chevy truck. When he called today, he was rude and obnoxious on the phone. So, I left him a little present as a reminder of his stinky attitude."

My eyes got wide. "You didn't! What did you do?"

He chuckled. "I put a nice piece of fish I saved from dinner under his seat. Let's see how long it takes for him to figure out where that awful smell is coming from!"

I put my hands on my hips. "Joey, that's not like you at all. What got into you?"

He winked at me. "You."

I shook my head, but I had to smile. Joey, who always let people walk all over him, was finding his own subtle ways to stand up for himself. I was proud of him.

"So, did you get your schedule for senior year?" he asked.

"Yup, right here." I handed him the yellow slip of paper and wrapped my apron around me.

He pulled the pen from behind his ear and almost—almost—put it in his mouth. I watched it as he aimed for his mouth, glanced at me, then replaced it behind his ear.

I smiled. "So, you can be taught. Good boy, Joey. I'm proud of you."

He shrugged. "Yeah, well, with you and Nisha yelling at me all the time about how gross it is, I guess I finally agree."

He opened my schedule and read it. "US history, calculus, gym, lunch, anatomy and physiology, Spanish, English, and FDA during study hall." He looked at me funny. "What's FDA?"

My cheeks grew hot. "Future Doctors of America. I decided I want to go to medical school. And I want to work with young cancer patients. There are plenty of good schools in New York and Pennsylvania that I could apply to and still be close to everyone here."

He took my hand and squeezed. "That's great! I'm so glad you decided to finish, but what made you decide to go to med school? And do you have the grades for it? I hear it's really hard to get in."

"My very recent hospital stay made the decision for me. And of course I have the grades. Don't you know by now how smart I am?"

He didn't dare argue with my logic. Guess he was pretty smart, too.

"And my doctor was very cute." I raised an eyebrow at him.

"Was he now?" He ripped his hand from mine. "Did you tell him you were taken?"

"Nope." His face fell. I grabbed his hand again. "But I didn't have to. When you left after visiting hours every day, he came in and said, 'You really like that guy, huh?' And I said yes."

I looked into those eyes, and as he stared back I knew that everything leading up to this moment had happened on purpose. I needed it all to get to where I was today. And where I would be in the future.

Autumn Rayne Taylor—devoted daughter, loyal girlfriend, lovable sister, future doctor.

The future never looked so good.

Acknowledgements

This book would not have been possible without the amazing support and love from so many people in my life.

Special thanks to my husband, Jed, for tolerating all the nights we ordered take-out so I could write. I know I never could have done this without you. You inspire me to be a better person every single day.

Thanks to my mom for believing in me and giving me unconditional love throughout my life. Your love means more to me than you will ever know. To my stepfather, Paul, for putting up with all the phone calls and lunches needed to discuss my journey to publication.

To my dad for instilling me with a love of travel and a curiosity about the world—these traits have helped me to be a better writer.

Thanks to my sister, Chrisy, for being my first beta reader and offering me great advice to improve my writing. If you hadn't forced me to read *Twilight*, I would not be where I am today. I miss you every single day I don't see you. To my brother-in-law, Jim, for putting up with me and letting me steal my sister away from you so many nights on the phone. Thanks to my niece, Jessica, for sharing your books with me and really "getting" me. I swear, in some far off alternate reality, we are twins!

Thanks to my brother, Scott, and his wife, Kelly, for cheering me on. To my niece and nephew, Isabel and Colin, for entertaining me and making me smile. I'm so happy you are all a part of my life.

Oma and Opa, your support and love throughout my life has meant a lot to me.

To my stepchildren, Ashley, Shane, and Jordan, who offered advice on the real life of teens today and also put up with take-out on many nights so I could write—I appreciate your help.

A huge shout out to Kate Kaynak and the team at Spencer Hill Press—especially Patricia Riley, Trisha Wooldridge, Rich Storrs, Kendra Saunders, Shira Lipkin, and all of the staff and interns who worked on *Triangles*—for taking on a new author and making me feel like family. With your help and guidance, this publishing adventure has been great, and *Triangles* has become the best book it could be!

To my cover designer, Vic Caswell, for spending many hours with me so we could come up with the perfect book cover—you nailed it!

Thanks to my beta readers—Jackie, Kim, and Laura—who read every chapter and offered great advice on how to improve *Triangles*. Sharing this journey with you has made it fun and exciting, and I hope we can all meet in real life one day.

Thanks to my critique group—Toni, Archana, Heather, Aideen, Carol, Christine, Leslie, and Patti—for your inspiration and friendship. I look forward to our monthly meetings and emails chock full of writing advice.

Thanks to my first grade teacher, Elaine, for teaching me how to read and write and cheering me on all these years later. I'd also like to thank all the great teachers I've had over the years—many of you inspired me and pushed me to do my best.

Thanks to my amazing travel agent, Sue, for booking a ton of great trips for me, especially the ones to Bermuda that inspired this story.

Thanks to Patrick at QueryTracker.net and all the writers on the forums for years of support, encouragement, and helpful information.

Thanks to Annie Bomke of ABLiterary who read the manuscript prior to publication and offered some great advice to make it better. Thanks to all the agents and editors who took the time to read my query or submissions and respond with a kind word. Those words, no matter how few, made me want to be a better writer.

To all my friends, extended family, and coworkers for listening to me talk about my book and for sharing in my excitement along the way—I'm honored and humbled to be surrounded by such wonderful people.

A special shout out to Kayleigh-Marie Gore of K-Books, for welcoming me into the world of book bloggers and sharing in my excitement about Triangles, and to all the book bloggers out there who love to read as much as I do, and who helped spread the word about *Triangles*.

Love to my three sweet cats who sit with me when I write and offer to help by stepping all over my keyboard.

And finally, thanks to everyone I have ever met who has, in some way, inspired me, encouraged me, supported me, or helped me. Life is hard enough, but with so many amazing people in the world, life is worth living.

THE DOLLHOUSE ASYLUM

When seventeen year old Cheyenne Laurent falls for Teo Richardson, she thinks the biggest problem is that he's a little too old for her, a little too mysterious and a lot too smart. But that's before he kisses her. Before the monsters start taking over the world. Before Teo takes her.

Cheyenne wakes up on a street lined with fourteen houses—seven on each side—clueless as to why she's there. She knocks on doors and soon learns that each house is filled with another teen—seven girls on one side, seven boys on the other—and no one is allowed to tell her anything. She has to figure out the truth herself. It's not until Teo reveals his intentions that she understands. He's created his own world, Elysian Fields, where everyone has asylum from the monsters and where Teo and Cheyenne can be together.

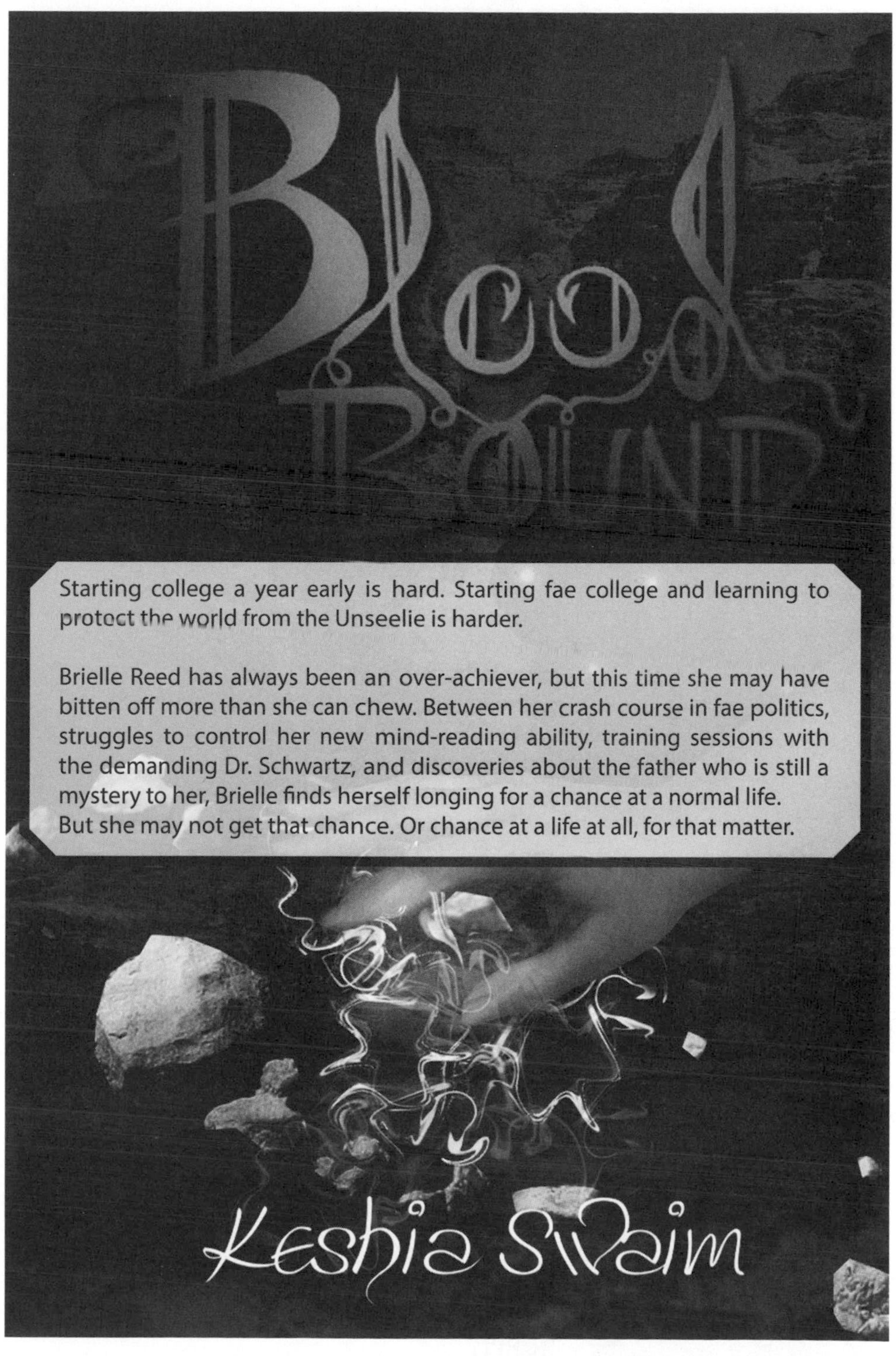
Blood Bound
Starting college a year early is hard. Starting fae college and learning to protect the world from the Unseelie is harder.
Brielle Reed has always been an over-achiever, but this time she may have bitten off more than she can chew. Between her crash course in fae politics, struggles to control her new mind-reading ability, training sessions with the demanding Dr. Schwartz, and discoveries about the father who is still a mystery to her, Brielle finds herself longing for a chance at a normal life.
But she may not get that chance. Or chance at a life at all, for that matter.
Keshia Swaim

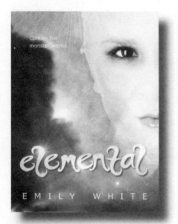

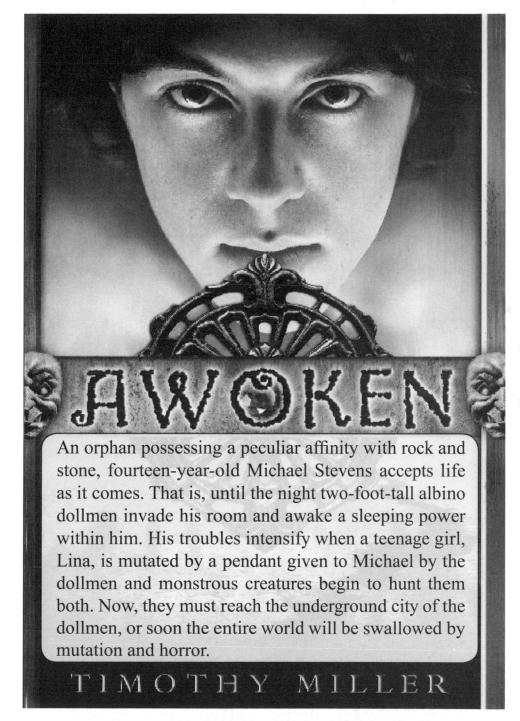

About the Author

Kimberly Miller received Bachelor's degrees from Georgian Court University and Rutgers University and a Master's degree from The University of Medicine and Dentistry of New Jersey. She is an avid reader and particularly enjoys true crime and young adult novels. She grew up in New Jersey and currently resides in Monmouth County with her husband and three cats. When she's not writing, she loves to travel to sunny islands where she snorkels by day and stargazes by night. She always takes her Nook with her.

For more information:
Twitter:@KimberlyAnnNJ
Blog: writersbytheshore.blogspot.com
Website: kimberlyannmiller.com